MY FATHER'S MOON

Elizabeth Jolley was born in the industrial Midlands of England in 1923. She moved to Western Australia in 1959 with her husband and three children. She has worked in a variety of occupations and is currently cultivating a small orchard and teaching part-time at Curtin University of Technology.

Elizabeth Jolley has been acclaimed as one of Australia's leading writers and received an AO for her contribution to Australian literature. She has had fiction and poetry published in Australian literary journals and anthologies, which, together with her plays, have been broadcast on British and Australian radio. She has published three collections of short fiction, and eight novels, of which *Mr Scobie's Riddle* won 'The Age' Book of the Year Award, *Milk and Honey* the NSW Premier's Award, and *The Well* the Miles Franklin Award.

Also by Elizabeth Jolley

Five Acre Virgin and other stories
The Travelling Entertainer and other stories
Palomino
The Newspaper of Claremont Street
Mr Scobie's Riddle
Woman in a Lampshade
Foxybaby
Milk and Honey
The Well
The Sugar Mother

MY FATHER'S MOON

Elizabeth Jolley

Penguin Books

Penguin Books Australia Ltd
487 Maroondah Highway, P.O. Box 257
Ringwood, Victoria, 3134, Australia
Penguin Books Ltd
Harmondsworth, Middlesex, England
Viking Penguin Inc.
40 West 23rd Street, New York, NY 10010, USA
Penguin Books Canada Limited
2801 John Street, Markham, Ontario, Canada, L3R 1B4
Penguin Books (N.Z.) Ltd
182-190 Wairau Road, Auckland 10, New Zealand

First published by Viking Australia, 1989
Published in Penguin, 1989

Typeset in Sabon by Southern Cross Typesetting, Keysborough, Vic
Made and printed in Australia by Australian Print Group, Maryborough, Australia.

CIP

Jolley, Elizabeth, 1923-
My father's moon.

ISBN 014 011125 5.

I. Title.

A823'.3

For Leonard Jolley

I would like to express my thanks to the Curtin University of Technology (formerly the Western Australian Institute of Technology) for the continuing privilege of being with students and colleagues in the School of Communication and Cultural Studies and for the provision of a room in which to write. I would like, in particular, to thank Don Watts, Peter Reeves, Brian Dibble and Don Grant.

A special thanks is offered to Nancy McKenzie who, for a great many years, has typed my manuscripts. Her patience is endless.

AUTHOR'S NOTE

It comes as a surprise to realize that time has gone by and that there are now people who are no longer familiar with the abbreviations which were once a part of everyday existence.

ATS was the abbreviation for Auxiliary Territorial Service. ARP stood for Air Raid Precaution, NA was Nursing Auxiliary (or sometimes Naughty Annie). The abbreviations were always used. They were part of the idiom. I never heard the words spoken in full. Similarly RMO and RSO were always said for the Resident Medical Officer and the Resident Surgical Officer respectively.

Elizabeth Jolley

FAIRFIELDS

'Why can't the father, the father of your – what I mean is why can't he do something?'

'I've told you, he's dead.'

'How can you say that, he was on the phone last night. I could tell by your voice, that's who it was.'

'He's dead. I've told you.'

At last the day has come when I must leave for Fairfields. It is all arranged. I have been there once already and know it to be a place of grated raw vegetables and children with restless eyes. It is also a place of poetry and music and of people with interesting lives and ideas.

'I simply can't understand you. How could you with your education and your background breed like a rabbit –'

'You're always saying that, for years you've said it. I've told you, rabbits have six, I only one.'

'How can you speak to me, your mother, like that.'

'Oh shut up and remember this. I'm never coming back. Never!'

'And another thing, Helena looks like a miner's child dressed up for an outing!' My mother does not like the white frock and the white socks and the white hair ribbons. I tie Helena's hair in two bunches with enormous bows and do not remind my mother that she bought the white frock, and the white socks

1

and the white ribbons.

'She'll get a headache, her hair pulled tight like that. And why white for a train journey, two train journeys. Oh Vera!' My mother, I can see, has tears in her eyes. 'Leave Helena here with me, your father and I would like to have her here with us, please! Besides, she is happy with us.'

But I will not be parted from my child. I throw a milk bottle across the kitchen, it shatters on the tiles and I am pleased because my mother is frightened. 'What's wrong with miners and their children and their outings?' I shout at her.

Perhaps Helena would be happier with her grandmother. I do not want to think this and it is painful to be told.

My father comes with us to the station.

'That's a nice coat,' he says, carrying it for me. It is my school winter coat, dark green and thick. It would not fit into my case so I have to carry it or wear it.

'It's a new coat, is it?' he says feeling the cloth with his hands. I don't reply because I have been wearing the coat for so many years.

We are too early for the train. The platform is deserted.

'It looks like a Loden,' he is still talking about the coat. 'Like an Austrian Loden cloth.' He is restless, my father, very white faced and he holds Helena's hand and walks up and down the platform, up and down. The coat on his other arm.

Always when my father sees off a train he is at the station too soon. And then, when the train is about to leave, when the whistle is being blown and the doors slam shut, one after the other down the whole length of the train, he rushes away and comes back with newspapers and magazines and pushes them through the window as he runs beside the now moving train. As the engine gets up steam and the carriages clank alongside the platform my father increases his speed, keeping up a smiling face outside the window.

His bent figure, his waving arms and his white face have always been the last things I have seen when leaving. I know too from being with him, seeing other people off, that he stands at the end of the platform, still waving, long after the train has disappeared.

Walking up and down we do not speak to each other. The smell of the station and the sound of an engine at the other platform remind me of Ramsden and of the night several years earlier when I met her train. Ramsden, staff nurse Ramsden, arriving at midnight. There was a thick fog and her train was delayed.

'I've invited Ramsden to come and stay for a few days,' I said to my mother then, assuming a nonchalance, a carelessness of speech to hide Ramsden's age and seniority.

'Why of course Vera, a nursing friend is always welcome ...' There had been a natural progression from school friend to nursing friend. My father never learned to follow, to keep up with this progression.

'And is Miss Ramsden a good girl?' would be his greeting, a continuation of, 'and is Jeanie a good girl?' He would say it to Ramsden without seeing the maturity and the elegance and without any understanding of the superior quality of her underclothes.

'My parents are looking forward to meeting you.' I invited Ramsden knowing already these other things.

Ramsden, with two tickets to Beethoven, in our Town Hall, prepared herself to make the long journey.

Putting off the visit, in my mind, from one day to the next, reluctantly, at last I was in the Ladies Only waiting room crouched over a dying fire, thin lipped and hostile with the bitter night. My school coat heavy but not warm enough and my shoes soaked.

Ramsden, who had once, unasked, played the piano for my tears, arrived at last. I could see she was cold. She was pale and there were dark circles of fatigue round her eyes. She came towards me distinguished in her well-cut tailored jacket and skirt. Her clothing and manner set her apart immediately from the other disembarking passengers.

'Miss Ramsden will have to share the room,' my mother said

3

before I left for the station, 'your sister's come home again.' Shrugging and blinking I went on reading without replying. Reading, getting ready slowly, turning the page of my book, keeping one finger in the page while I dressed to go and meet the train.

Ramsden came towards me with both hands reaching out in leather gloves. At once she was telling me about the Beethoven, the choral symphony, and how she had been able to get tickets. There was Bach too, Cantata eighteen. Remember? she said. *For as the rain cometh down and the snow from heaven,* she, beating time with one hand, sang, *so shall my word be that goeth forth out of my mouth* ... In the poor light of the single mean lamp her eyes were pools of pleasure and tenderness. She did not mind the black-out she said when I apologized for the dreariness of the station. 'Ramsden,' I said, 'I'm most awfully sorry but there's been something of a tragedy at home. I couldn't let you know ... I'm so most awfully sorry ...'

'Not ...?' Concern added more lines to Ramsden's tired face. I nodded turning away from the smell of travelling which hung about the woollen cloth of her suit.

'Oh Wright! I am so sorry, Veronica.' It was the first time she had spoken my first name, well almost the first time. I glanced at her luggage which stood by itself on the fast emptying platform. The case seemed to hold in its shape and leather the four long hours of travelling, the long tedious journey made twice as long by the fog.

There would be a stopping train to London coming through late, expected at three in the morning the porter said as Ramsden retrieved her case from its desolation.

A glance into the waiting room showed that the remnant of the fire was now a little heap of cold ash. Perhaps, she suggested, even though there was no fire it would be warmer to sit in there.

'I'm so sorry,' I said, 'I shall not be able to wait for your train.' So sorry, I told her, I must get back, simply must get back.

'Is it ...?' More concern caused Ramsden to raise her dark

4

eyebrows. The question unfinished, I drew my arm away from her hand's touch. I thought of the needlework and embroidery book I had chosen from her room, too nervous with my act, then, to read the titles when, to please me, she said to choose a book to have to keep, as a present, from her shelf. The badly chosen book I thought, at the time, made me feel sick. I began that day, almost straight away, to feel sick.

We walked along the fog-filled platform. 'I've come to you all the way from London,' Ramsden, drawing me to her, began in her low voice. 'I'd hoped ...' I turned away from the clumsy embrace of her breathed-out whispered words knowing her breath to be the breath of hunger.

'I'm sorry,' I said again stiffening away from her, 'but I'll have to go.'

'To them,' she said, 'yes of course, you must.' She nodded her understanding and her resignation.

'I am sorry I can't wait till your train comes. I can't wait with you. I'm most awfully sorry!' Trying to change, to lift my accent to match hers.

She nodded again. I knew from before, though I couldn't see them, what her eyes would be like.

I had to walk the three miles home as there were no buses at that time of night. The fog swirled cold in my face. The way was familiar but other things were not. My own body, for one thing, for I was trying, every day, to conceal my morning sickness.

I turn away trying to avoid the place on the platform where Ramsden tried to draw me towards an intensity of feeling I could not be a part of that night.

'She wasn't on the train,' I told my mother the next morning standing on purpose behind her flowered overall and keeping to the back of her head which was still encased in metal rollers. She was hurrying to get to the Red Cross depot. Her war effort.

'It was a dreadful night for travelling,' my mother said, not turning from the sink, 'perhaps your Miss Ramsden will send a letter. You can invite her again, perhaps in the spring, we'll have more space then, perhaps by then your sister will be better.'

My father, running now beside the moving train, pushes a magazine and a comic through the window. I, because I feel I must, lean out and see him waving at the end of the platform. Helena, clinging to my skirt, cries for her Grandpa.

Unable to stop thinking of Ramsden I wonder why do I think of her today after all this time of forgetting her. I never write to her. I never did write even when she wrote to me saying that she was still nursing and that she lived out, that she had a little flat which had escaped the bombs and if I liked to stay she would love to have me stay as long as I liked, 'as long as you feel like it'. I never answered. Never told her I had a child. Never let her into my poverty and never let her into my loneliness.

London is full of people who seem to know where they are and to have some purpose in this knowing. I drag my case and the coat and Helena and change stations and at last we are travelling through the fields and summer meadows of Hertfordshire. The train, this time, is dirty and has no corridor and immediately Helena wants the lavatory. I hate the scenery.

At last we are climbing the steep field path from the bus stop to the school. Fairfields, I have been there once already and know the way. The path is a mud path after it leaves the dry narrow track through the tall corn which is turning, waving and rippling, from the green to gold, spotted scarlet with poppies and visited by humming hot-weather insects. I have seen before that the mud is caused by water seeping from two enormous manholes in the trees at the top of the hill. Drains, the drains of Fairfields School.

'Who is that?' Helena stops whimpering. And I see a man standing quite still, half hidden by trees. He does not seem to be watching, rather it is as if he is trying to be unseen as we climb together. He does not move except to try and merge into a tree trunk. With the case I push Helena on up the steepest part of the path and I do not look back into the woods.

In the courtyard no one is about except for a little boy standing in the porch. He tells me his Granny will be coming to this door, that he is waiting to be fetched by her. 'My Granny's got a gas stove,' he tells me. I think suddenly of my mother's kitchen and wish that I could wait now at this door for her to come and fetch me and Helena. Straight away I want to go back.

Miss Palmer, the Principal, the one they call Patch, I know this too from my earlier visit, carrying a hod of coke, comes round from an outhouse.

'Ah!' she says. 'I see you mean to stay!' She indicates my winter coat. 'So this is Helena!' She glances at my child. 'She's buttoned up I daresay.' I know this to mean something not quite explained but I nod and smile. Patch tells me that no one is coming to fetch Martin. 'He's new, he hasn't,' she says, 'adjusted yet.'

She shows me my room which I am to share with Helena. It is bare except for a cupboard and two small beds. It is bright yellow with strong smelling distemper. There is a window, high up, strangled with creeper.

'Feel free to wander,' Patch says, 'tea in the study at four. Children's tea in the playroom at five and then the bathings. Paint the walls if you feel creative.' She has a fleshy face and short, stiff hair, grey like some sort of metal. I do not dislike her.

'Thank you,' I say, narrowing my eyes at the walls as if planning an exotic mural.

Helena, pulling everything from the unlocked case, intones a monologue over her rediscovered few toys. I stare into the foliage and the thick mass of summer green leaf immediately outside the window.

Later the Swiss girl, Josepha, who has the room opposite mine, takes me round the upstairs rooms which are strewn with sleeping children. We pull some of them out of bed and sit them

7

on little chipped enamel pots. There is the hot smell of sleeping children and their pots.

Josepha tells me the top bathroom is mine and she gives me a bath list. The face flannels and towels hang on hooks round the room.

Josepha comes late to breakfast and takes most of the bread and the milk and the butter up to her room where her sweetheart, Rudi, sleeps. I heard their endless talk up and down in another language, the rise and fall of an incomprehensible muttering all night long, or so it seemed in my own sleeplessness.

The staff sit at breakfast in a well-bred studied shabbiness huddled round a tall copper coffee pot and some blue bowls of milk. Children are not allowed and it seems that I hear Helena crying and crying locked in our room upstairs. Patch does not come to breakfast but Myles, who is Deputy Principal, fetches prunes and ryvita for her. She is dark-eyed and expensively dressed like Ramsden but she has nothing of Ramsden's music and tenderness. She is aloof and flanked by two enormous dogs. She is something more than Deputy Principal. Josepha explains.

'Do not go in,' Josepha points at Patch's door, 'if both together are in there.'

When I dress Helena I take great trouble over her hair ribbons and let her, with many changes of mind, choose her dress because I am sorry for leaving her alone, locked in to cry in a strange place. I have come to Fairfields to work with the idea that it will give Helena school and companionship and already I have tried to persuade her, to beg her and finally rushed away from her frightened crying because staff offspring (Myles' words) are not allowed at staff meals. I take a long time dressing Helena and find that Josepha has dressed all the children from my list as well as her own. I begin to collect up the little pots.

'No! Leave!' Josepha shouts and, tying the last child into a pinafore, she herds them downstairs. Moving swiftly Josepha can make me, with Helena clinging to my dress, seem useless.

Josepha does the dining room and I am to do, with Olive

Morris, the playroom where the smaller children have their meals. Mrs Morris has a little boy called Frank but Helena will not sit by him. She follows me with a piece of bread and treacle and I have to spend so much time cleaning her that Olive Morris does the whole breakfast and wipes the tables and the floor. She does not say anything only gets on with ladling cod-liver oil, which is free, into the children as they leave the little tables.

I discover that Olive Morris has three children in the school and that Josepha feels it is morally right that Olive should work more than anyone else because of this. Josepha is always dragging children off to have their hair washed. She has enormous washing days and is often scrubbing something violently at ten o'clock at night. The smell of scorching accompanies the fierceness of her ironing.

'Do not go in there,' she points to the first-floor bathroom, 'when Patch and Tanya are in there and,' she says, 'do not tell Myles!'

Tanya teaches art. She looks poor but Josepha says she is filthy rich and wears rags on purpose.

Tanya, on my first day, was painting headless clowns on the dining-room walls. She stepped back squinting at her work. 'They are going to play ball with the heads,' she explained bending down over her paint pots as if she had been talking to me for years.

'What a good idea,' I said, ashamed of my accent and trying to sound as if I knew all about painting.

That day she asked me what time it was, saying that she must hurry and get her wrists slashed before Frederick comes back from his holiday.

Later, in the pantry, she is there with both arms bandaged. 'Frederick the Great,' she says, 'he'll be back. Disinfectant, fly spray, cockroach powder and mouse traps. He will,' she says, 'ask you to examine his tonsils.'

Olive Morris looks ill. Sometimes when I sit in my room at night with an old cardigan round the light to keep it off Helena's bed I think of Olive and begin to understand what real poverty is; her dreadful little bowls of never clean washing, the rags which she is forever mending and her pale crumpled face from which her worried eyes look out hopelessly.

I have plenty of pretty clothes for Helena. And then it suddenly comes to me that this is the only difference. My prospects are the same as Olive's. I have as little hope for the future as she has. It just happens that at present, because of gifts from my mother, Helena, for the first years of her life, has been properly fed and is well dressed.

One hot afternoon I sit with the children in the sand pit hoping that they will play. There are only two little spades and the children quarrel and fight and bite each other. It is hard to understand why the children can't enjoy the spacious lawns and the places where they can run and shout and hide among the rose bushes. Beyond the lawn is deep uncut grass bright with buttercups and china-blue hare-bells. I am tired, tired in a way which makes me want to lie down in the long grass and close my eyes. Helena, crying, will not let me rest. The children are unhappy. I think it is because they do not have enough food. They are hungry all the time.

I do lie down and I look up at the sky. Once I looked at the sky, not with Ramsden but after we had been talking together. I would like to hear Ramsden's voice now. It is strange to wish this after so long. Perhaps it is because everyone here seems to have someone. Relationships, as they are called here, are acceptable. And I, having no one, wishing for someone, vividly recall Ramsden. She said, that time in the morning before I went for my day off to sleep among the spindles of rosemary at the end of my mother's garden, that love was infinite. That it was possible, if a person loved, to believe in the spiritual understanding of truths which were not fully understood intellectually. She said that the person you loved was not an end in itself, was not something you came to the end of, but was the beginning of discoveries which could be made because of loving someone.

Lying in the grass, pushing Helena away, I think about this

and wonder how I can bring it into the conversation at the four o'clock staff tea and impress Patch and Myles. I practise some words and an accent of better quality.

Because of being away from meadow flowers for so long I pick some buttercups and some of the delicate grasses adding their glowing tips to the bunch wondering, with bitter uneasiness, how I can get them unseen to my room. I can see Patch and Myles at the large window of Patch's room. Instead of impressing them I shall simply seem vulgar, acquisitive and stupid, clutching a handful of weeds, ineffectually shepherding the little children towards their meagre plates of lettuce leaves and Patch-rationed bread.

In the evening there is a thunder storm with heavy rain. I am caught in the rain on the way back from the little shop where I have tried to buy some fruit. The woman there asks me if I am from the school and if I am, she says, she is unable to give me credit. In the shop there is the warm sweet smell of newspapers, firelighters and cheap sweets, aniseed, a smell of ordinary life which is missing in the life of the school. Shocked I tell her I can pay and I buy some poor-quality carrots as the apples, beneath their rosy skins, might be rotten. I will wash the carrots and give them to Helena when I have to leave her alone in our room in the mornings.

The storm is directly overhead, the thunder so loud I am afraid Helena will wake and be frightened so I do not shelter in the shop but hurry back along the main road, through the corn and up the steep path. I am wet through and the mud path is a stream. The trees sway and groan. I slip and catch hold of the undergrowth to stop myself from falling. When I look up I see that there is someone standing, half hidden, quite near, in the same place where a man was standing on that first afternoon. This man, I think it is the same man, is standing quite still letting the rain wash over him as it pours through the leaves and branches. His hair is plastered wet-sleeked on his round head and water runs in rivulets down his dark suit. He, like me, has no coat. He does not move and he does not speak.

He seems to be looking at me as I try to climb the steep path as quickly as I can. I feel afraid. I have never felt or experienced fear like this before. Real terror, because of his stillness, makes my legs weak. I hurry splashing across the courtyard and make my way, trembling, round to the kitchen door. Wet and shivering I meet Olive Morris in the passage outside my room. She is carrying a basin of washing. Rags trail over her shoulder and her worn-out blouse, as usual, has come out of her skirt.

I tell her about the man in the woods. 'Ought I to tell Patch?' I try to breathe calmly. 'It's getting dark out there. He's soaked to the skin. I ought to tell Patch.'

Olive Morris's shapeless soft face is paler than ever and her lips twitch. She looks behind her nervously.

'No,' she says in a low voice. 'No, never tell anyone here anything. Never!' She hurries off along to the other stairs which lead directly up to her room in the top gable of the house.

While I am drying my hair, Olive Morris, in a torn raincoat, comes to my door.

'I'm going down to post a letter,' she says putting a scarf over her head. 'So if I see your stranger in the trees I'll send him on his way – there's no need at all to have Myles go out with the dogs. No need at all.'

My surprise at the suggestion that Myles and the dogs might hunt the intruder is less than the feeling of relief that I need not go to Patch's room where Myles, renowned for her sensitive nudes, will be sketching Patch in charcoal and reading poetry aloud. They would smile at each other, exchanging intimate glances while only half listening to what I had to say. Earlier, while Patch pretended to search her handbag for a ten shilling note as part of the payment owing to me, Myles had looked up gazing as if thoughtfully at me for a few minutes and then had resumed her reading of the leather-bound poems.

Josepha is on bedroom duty and the whole school is quiet. Grateful that Helena has not been disturbed by the storm I lie down in my narrow bed.

Instead of falling asleep I think of the school and how it is not at all as I thought it would be. Helena stands alone all day peering through partly closed doors watching the dancing classes. She looks on at the painting and at the clay-modelling and is only on the edge of the music.

There must be people who feel and think as I do but they are not here as I thought they would be. I want to lean out of a window in a city full of such people and call to some passer-by. I am by my own mistakes buried in this green-leafed corruption and I am alone.

My day off which Josepha did not tell me about till all the children were washed and dressed was a mixture of relief and sadness. A bus ride to town. Sitting with Helena in a small cafe eating doughnuts. Choosing a sun hat for Helena. Buying some little wooden spades and some coloured chalks. Trying to eat a picnic lunch of fruit and biscuits on a road mender's heap of gravel chips. I can hardly bear to think about it. As I handed Helena her share and saw her crouched on the stones with her small hands trying to hold her food without a plate I knew how wrong it was that she was like this with no place to go home to.

I think now over and over again that it is my fault that we are alone, more so than ever, at the side of the main road with cars and lorries streaming in both directions.

There is a sudden sound, a sound of shooting. Gun shots. I go into the dark passage. From Josepha's room comes the usual running up and down of their voices, first hers and then his. I am afraid to disturb them. A door further down clicks open and I see, with relief, it is Tanya.

'Oh it's you Tanya! Did you hear anything just now?'

'Lord no. I never hear a thing m'dear and I never ask questions either so if you've been letting anyone in or out I just wouldn't know darling.'

I tell her about the shot.

'Lord!' Tanya says. 'That's Frederick. Back from his leave. Frederick the Great, literature and drama. Room's over the stables. Never unpacks. Got a Mother. North London. Cap gun. Shoots off gun for sex. The only trouble is darling,' Tanya drawls, 'the orgasm isn't shared.' She disappears into the bathroom saying that she's taken an overdose and so must have her bath quickly.

I go on up the next lot of stairs to Olive's room. I have never been there. I must talk to someone. Softly I knock on the door. At once Olive opens it as if she is waiting on the other side of it.

'Oh it's you!' Her frightened white face peers at me.

'Can I come in?' I step past her hesitation into her room. It is not my intention to be rude, I tell her, it is my loneliness. Olive catches me by the arm. Her eyes implore. I am suddenly ashamed for, sitting up in bed wearing a crumpled shirt and a tie, is a man. The man I had seen standing with sinister patience in the rain.

'Oh Olive, I am so sorry. I do beg ...'

'This is Mr Morris, my husband. This is Vera Wright, dear,' Olive whispers a plain introduction.

'Pleased to meet you I'm sure,' Mr Morris says. I continue to mumble words of apology and try to move backwards to the door.

The three Morris children are all in a heap asleep in a second sagging double bed up against the gable window. Washing is hanging on little lines across the crowded room and Mr Morris's suit is spread over the bed ends to dry.

'Mr Morris is on his way to a business conference,' Olive begins to explain. I squeeze her arm. 'I'll see you tomorrow,' I say. We are wordless at the top of the steep stairs. She is tucking her blouse into her too loose skirt. It seems to me that she will go on performing this little action forever even when she has no clothes on.

'No one at all knows that Mr Morris is here,' she says in a breaking whisper.

At breakfast I wish I had someone to whom I could carry, with devotion, bread and butter and coffee. I could not envy Myles because of Patch, or Josepha because of Rudi. Tanya must be feeling as I feel for she prepares a little tray for Frederick and is back almost at once with a swollen bruised bleeding nose and quite quickly develops two black eyes which, it is clear, will take days to fade.

It would be nice for Olive to sail into breakfast and remove a quantity of food bearing it away with dignity to the room in the top gable.

'I suppose you know,' I say to Patch when we meet by chance in the hall, 'that Olive Morris's husband arrived unexpectedly last night and will be with us for a few days.'

Patch says, 'Is he dear?' That is all.

Mr Morris, who is a big man, wears his good suit every day thus setting himself somewhat apart from the rest of us. He comes to supper and tells us stories about dog racing. His dogs win. He tells us about boxing and wrestling. He has knocked out all the champs. He knows all their names and the dates of the matches. He knows confidence men who treble their millions in five minutes. His brothers and sisters teach in all the best universities and his dear old mother is the favourite Lady in Waiting at Buckingham Palace. Snooker is his forte, a sign, he tells us, of a misspent youth. He sighs.

Patch comes to supper every night. Josepha stops shouting at Olive. Mr Morris calls Olive 'Lovey' and reminds her, for us all to hear, of extravagant incidents in their lives. He boasts about his older children regaling us with their exam results and sporting successes. Olive withers. She is smaller and paler and trembles visibly when Patch, in a genial mood, with mockery and amusement in her voice, leads Mr Morris into greater heights of story telling. While he talks his eyes slide sideways as he tries to observe us all and see the effects of his fast-moving mouth.

Mr Morris, we have to see, is the perfect husband and father. During the day he encourages his children and the other children to climb all over him. He organizes games and races,

15

promising prizes.

He gives all sorts of presents, the table in the kitchen is heaped with chickens and ducks, ready for the oven, jars of honey and expensive jams and baskets of apples and fresh vegetables. Patch prepares the meals herself. Our vegetarian diet was only because the local butchers, unpaid, no longer supply the school.

Frederick, refusing to come to meals, refusing to leave the loft, has a bucket on a string into which Josepha, he will not take from anyone else, puts chicken breasts and bread and butter and a white jug of milk. Tanya says if there is any wormy fruit or fly-blown meat Frederick the Great will get it. He, she explains, because of always searching for them, attracts the disasters in food.

'Where is Mr Philbrick?' Patch asks correcting quickly what she calls a fox's paw, a slip of the tongue. 'Mr Morris? Why isn't he here?' She is carving, with skill, the golden chickens and Myles is serving the beans and baby carrots which shine in butter. Olive can hardly swallow a mouthful.

'What's keeping Mr Morris?' I ask her loud enough for Patch's ears. 'Anything wrong?' devouring my plateful. 'Is someone ill?'

'No. No – it's nothing at all,' she whispers.

Towards the end of the meal Mr Morris comes in quietly and sits down next to the shrinking Olive. Patch, with grease on her large chin, hands a plate of chicken to him. Thick-set, stockily at the head of the table, she sings contralto as if guarding a secret with undisturbed complacence.

There is a commotion in the hall and the sound of boots approaching.

'It is the Politz!' Josepha, on bedroom duty, calls from the stairs.

Mr Morris leaps up.

'Leave this to me dear Lady,' he says to Patch. And, with a snake-like movement, he is on his way to the door.

We follow just in time to see Mr Morris, suddenly small and

white-faced, being led in handcuffs to the front door and out to a car which, with the engine running, is waiting.

I want to say something to Olive to comfort her.

'It's better this way,' she says, 'better for him this way, better than them getting him with dogs. And the children,' she says, 'they didn't see anything.' I don't ask her what Mr Morris has done. She does not tell me anything except that Mr Morris finds prison life unbearable and that he has a long stretch of it ahead.

Patch walks about the school singing and eating the ends off a crusty loaf. When the bills come addressed to her for all the presents from Mr Morris she laughs and tosses them into the kitchen fire.

One of the little boys rushing through the hall stops to glance at Tanya's latest painting.

'How often do you have sexual intercourse?' he pauses long enough in his flight to ask.

'Three times a week.' Tanya steps back to squint at her work. 'Never more, never less,' she says.

Tanya says that Frederick the Great is coming down from the loft and will be at supper. I wash my hair and put on my good dress and go down to the meal early rejoicing that it is Olive's night to settle the children. I am looking forward to meeting Frederick. Perhaps, at last, there will be someone for me. Olive scuttles by with her tray which she must eat upstairs. I hear the uproar from the bedrooms and smile to myself.

Frederick is bent in a strange contortion over the sink in the pantry. He is trying to see into his throat with a torch and a small piece of broken mirror stuck into the loose window frame. I am glad to be able to meet him without Josepha and Tanya.

'Would you mind looking at my throat,' he says straightening up. He is very tall and his eyes enclosed in gold-rimmed spectacles do not look at me. 'I've been trying a new gargle.' He hands me the torch and I peer into his throat.

'Is is painful?' I feel I should ask him.

'Not at all,' he says, taking back the torch.

In the dining room Frederick has a little table to himself in the corner. He eats alone quickly and leaves at once. I sit in my usual place. One of the children is practising on the pantry piano. I listen to the conscientious stumblings. Ramsden played Bach seriously repeating and repeating until she was satisfied and then moving on to the next phrases.

In my head I compose a letter to Ramsden ... *this neck of the woods*, this is not my way but it persists, *this neck of the woods is not far from London. Any chance of your coming down one afternoon? Staff tea is at four. I'd love to see you and show you round* ...

There is so much I would tell Ramsden.

For as the rain cometh down, and the snow from heaven, and returneth
not thither, but watereth the earth, and make it bring
forth and bud,
that it may give seed to the sower, and bread to the eater:
so shall my word be that goeth forth out of my mouth:

I want to write to Ramsden. After that night and after almost five years how do I address her? Dear Ramsden? Dear staff nurse Ramsden? She might be Sister Ramsden. She might not be nursing now though she did go on after the end of the war. She might be married though I think that is unlikely, perhaps she is on concert platforms ...

Dear Ramsden I have no way at all of getting away from this place. Please Ramsden can you come? Please?

Patch and Myles come in to supper. Ignoring me they devotedly help each other to mountains of grated raw carrots and cabbage.

MY FATHER'S MOON

Before this journey is over I intend to speak to the woman. *Ramsden*, I shall say, *is it you?* The train has just left the first station, there is plenty of time in which to contemplate the conversation; the questions and the answers and the ultimate revelation. It is comfortable to think about the possibilities.

The woman sitting on the other side, diagonally opposite, could be someone I used to know. A long time ago. In another place. Her clothes are of the same good quality, the same materials, even the same colours. It is the tilt of the head which is so remarkably similar. She looks like someone who is passionately fond of the cello. Fond of listening to the cello. I look at her hands and feel sure she plays the piano. When I look at her hands it is as if I can hear her playing a Mozart sonata or practising something from Bach. Repeating and repeating phrases until a perfection is achieved. I am certain, as I go on looking, that she plays Cyril Scott's *Water Wagtail*.

For some time now I have travelled by suburban train to and from the places where I work. This evening I am on the earlier train. I caught the earlier train on purpose even though, because of this, I arrive too soon ...

The unfamiliar early train travels, of course, through the same landscape, the familiar. There is nothing remarkable in this. It is my reason for taking this train which makes the

19

journey remarkable. The train stops at the same stations but naturally the people getting in or out are not the same people as those on the later train.

I sit staring out of the window at the same meeting places of unknown roads, at the backs of the same shabby houses and garden fences, at the same warehouses and the same smash repair yards and at the now well-known backs of the metropolitan markets.

About once a week I catch the earlier train for a special reason. Every week it is the same. Every week I think that this time I will speak to her. This week I am on this train in order to speak to her. I will cross from my seat and sit by her and I will speak to her. I always sit where I can see her from the side and from the back and I sit close enough to hear her voice if she should speak. I long to hear the voice, her voice, to know whether it is the same voice. Voices and ways of speaking often remain unchanged.

This time I almost brought the violin case with me though I am not now accustomed to carrying it when I go out. If Ramsden saw the violin case, if the woman saw it, she would remember.

'They're both in good condition,' the man in the shop said. 'Both the same price. Choose your pick,' he said. 'Take your time.'

I could not make up my mind, and then I chose the violin case. The following week I went back for the camera case but it had gone. The violin case had once been lined with some dark red soft material, some of it was still left. I only opened it once and it was then I saw the remains of the lining. I carried the case whenever I went out.

The first time I saw Ramsden the sentry at the hospital gates had his bayonet fixed. He looked awkward and he blushed as he said, 'Who goes there!' Surprised, I told him my name and my identity-card number, it was the middle of the morning and we were challenged, as a rule, only after dark. I supposed the rule must have been changed. A despatch from H.Q., I thought, seeing in my mind the nimble motor cyclist arrive.

Ramsden, on her way out, gave a small smile in the direction of the violin case and I was pleased that I had bought it. On that day I had been at the hospital for seven weeks.

Two people sitting behind me are talking in German. I begin to listen to the animated conversation and grope for meanings in what they are saying in this language which was once familiar. I begin to recognize a few words: *eine Dame... keine Ahnung...langsam... Milch und Tränenbäche...mein Elend...zu grosser Schmerz und so weiter.* But I want the words of cherishing spoken in German. I want those first words the child remembers on waking to the knowing of language. I wish now in the train to be spoken to as *du*...

The woman sitting on the other side is looking calmly out of the window. Naturally she sees the same things that I see. It is quite comfortable to know that I have only to lean over and touch her sleeve.

I never worked with Ramsden. I saw her sometimes in the dining room. There are several little pictures of her in my mind. The doctors called her Miss Ramsden. She did the penicillin syringes too. One nurse, usually a senior, spent the whole day cleaning and sterilizing the syringes and the needles, setting up the trolley, giving the injections and then clearing the trolley and cleaning and sterilizing and checking all over again. Whenever I passed the glass doors of the ward where she was I saw her in the sterilizing room seriously attending to the syringes and needles for the three-hourly injections.

'Ramsden,' I said, 'this is the part we like isn't it? This part, this is it, we like this ...'

'It's the anticipation,' she replied, 'it's what is hoped for and then realized.' She was sitting on the edge of her bed.

'This part, this ...' I said once more. I pointed with one finger as if to place the cello somewhere in the space between us. 'This going down part,' I said, 'is the part we like best.'

Ramsden nodded. She was mending a stocking. Her stockings were not the usual ones, not the grey uniform stockings which were lisle and, after repeated washing, were hard to mend. Ramsden's stockings, I noticed immediately, were smooth and soft and they glistened like honey. Dark, honey-coloured stockings. Ramsden's stockings were silk stockings. She was oversewing a run at the ankle. Her sewing was done so carefully I knew the repair would be invisible. She had invited me into her room to listen to a record.

'Do you know why you like it?' she repeated an earlier question. The cello reminded me of her. How could I tell her this. I shook my head. Staff nurse Ramsden, she was senior to me. When she listened to music she sat with her legs crossed over and she moved her foot very slightly, I could see, in time to the music. How could I speak to her about the downward thrust of the cello and about the perfection in the way the other instruments came up to meet the cello. How could I say to her that I thought someone had measured the movement of the notes controlling carefully the going down and the coming up in order to produce this exquisite mixture. There were other things too that I could not speak about. How could I say to her what I thought about the poet Rilke, about his face and about how I felt when I looked at his photograph in the book she had. She knew his poems, understood them. I wanted to tell her that when I looked at Rilke's face I felt clumsy as if made of wood. Even the way he stood in the photograph had something special about it and when I read a poem of his to myself I wanted to read lines aloud to her. 'Listen to this, Ramsden,' I wanted to say, 'listen to this.'

But hand in hand now with that God she walked,
her paces circumscribed by lengthy shroudings
uncertain, gentle, and without impatience.
Wrapt in herself, like one whose time is near ...

There were other things too from *Orpheus*, but she knowing his

22

poems might have felt I was intruding. When I read Rilke everything I was trying to write seemed commonplace and unmusical, completely without any delicacy and refinement. I never told Ramsden I was trying to write because what I wrote was about her. I wanted to write about Ramsden. How could I tell her that?

Later when she talked about the music she said the soloist was innocent and vulnerable. She said the music was eloquent and that there was something intimate about the cello. She was very dignified and all her words seemed especially chosen. I wanted her to say them all again to me. The word intimate, I had never before spoken to anyone who used this word. She said the cello, the music of the cello, was intimate. Ramsden's discipline prevented her from repeating what she had said. She continued to oversew her stocking and we listened once more to the second movement. When I listened to a particular passage in this movement I seemed to see Ramsden walking ahead of me with great beech trees on either side of her. Magnificent smooth trees with their rain-soaked branches darkened and dripping. Then we were walking together, I imagined, beneath these trees, with the wet leaves deep round our ankles. Ramsden, I thought, would have small ribbed socks on over her stockings ...

Lyrical, she said the music was lyrical and I was not sure what she meant. She said then that, if I liked, I could borrow her records.

When I played the record at home my father, not knowing the qualities of the cello, asked if I could make the music a bit quieter. It was my day off, most of it had been wasted because I slept and no one woke me. My father asked was there a piano piece, he said he liked the piano very much. I told him that staff nurse Ramsden played the piano and my mother said perhaps Miss Ramsden would come some time and play the piano for us. She said she would make a fire in the front room and we could all sit and listen ...

Because I caught the earlier train I have an hour to spare before it is time for the clinic to open. The people who attend this clinic will be setting off from their houses in order to keep their appointments.

I walk to a bus stop where there is a bench and, though I am in a familiar place, I feel as if I have come to a strange land. In one sense there is a strangeness because all the old houses and their once cared for gardens have gone. In their place are tall concrete buildings, floor upon floor of offices, all faced with gleaming windows. Some lit up and some dark. The buildings rise from parking lots all quite similar but unrecognizable as though I have never seen them before. Small trees and bushes planted as ornaments offer a few twigs and leaves. The new buildings are not at peace with their surroundings. They are not part of the landscape, they are in imposition. They do not match each other and they have taken away any tranquillity, any special quality of human life the streets may have had once.

The Easter lilies, uncherished, appear as they do every year with surprising suddenness, their pink and white long-lasting freshness bursting out of the brown, bald patches of earth at the ends of those places which have been left out from the spreading bitumen.

If I had spoken in the train I could have said, 'Ramsden,' I could have said, 'I feel sad. Lately I seem unable to prevent a feeling of melancholy which comes over me as soon as I wake up. I feel nervous and muddled and everything is accompanied by a sense of sorrow and futility.' Should I join a sect? I could have asked her. A cult? On TV these people, with a chosen way, all look light hearted. They dance carrying bricks and mortar across building sites. They jive and twist and break-dance from kitchens to dining rooms carrying wooden platters of something fresh and green neatly chopped up. Perhaps it is uncooked spinach. Perhaps it is their flying hair and their happy eyes which attract, but then the memory of the uneasiness of communal living and the sharing of possessions and money seems too difficult, too frightening to contemplate. In real life it won't, I could have told her, it won't be the same as it is on TV. Probably only the more sparkling members of the sect are filmed, I could have said this too, and something is sure to be painted on the spinach to make it look more attractive. Food in advertisements, I could have been knowledgeable, food in advertisements is treated before being photographed. I left the train at my station without another glance in her direction.

Perhaps the lilies are a reminder and a comfort. Without fail they flower at Easter. Forgotten till they flower, an unsought simultaneous caution and blessing.

It seems to me now, when I think of it, that my father was always seeing me off either at a bus stop or at the station. He would suggest that he come to the bus or the train just as I was about to leave. Sometimes he came part of the way in the train getting out at the first stop and then, waiting alone, he would travel on the first train back. Because of the decision being made at the last minute, as the train was moving, he would have only a platform ticket so, as well as all the waiting and the extra travelling, he would be detained at the other end to make explanations and to pay his fare for both directions. All this must have taken a lot of time. And sometimes in the middle of winter it was bitterly cold.

The strong feeling of love which goes from the parent to the child does not seem a part of the child which can be given back to the parent. I realize now with regret that I never thought then of his repeated return journeys. I never thought of the windswept platforms, of the small smouldering waiting-room fires and the long, often wet, walks from the bus to the house. I simply always looked ahead, being already on my journey even before I set out, to the place to which I was going.

The minutes which turned out to be the last I was to have with my father were at a railway station. When it was time for my train to leave even when the whistle was being blown my father went on with what he was saying. He said that if we never saw each other again I must not mind. He was getting older he said then, he was surprised at how quickly he was getting older and though he planned to live a long time it might be that we should not be able to make the next journeys in time. It is incredible that I could have paid so little attention then and the longing to hear his voice once more at this moment is something I never thought of till now.

He had his umbrella with him and when the train began to move he walked beside the moving train for as long as he could waving the umbrella. I did not think about the umbrella then either. But now I remember that during the years he often left it in trains and it travelled the length and breadth of England coming back at intervals labelled from Liverpool, Norfolk, St Ives and Glasgow to the lost-property office where he was, with a kind of apologetic triumph, able to claim it.

The huge Easter moon, as if within arm's length, as if it can be reached simply by stretching out both hands to take it and hold it, is low down in the sky, serene and full, lighting the night so that it looks as if everything is snow covered, and deep shadows lie across pale, moon-whitened lawns. This moon is the same moon that my father will have seen. He always told me when I had to leave for school, every term when I wept because I did not want to leave, he told me that if I looked at the moon, wherever I was, I was seeing the same moon that he was looking at. 'And because of this,' he said, 'you must know that I am not very far away. You must never feel lonely,' he said. He said the moon would never be extinguished. Sometimes, he said, it was not possible to see the moon, but it was always there. He said he liked to think of it as his.

I waited once for several hours at a bus stop, a temporary stop on a street corner in London. There was a traffic diversion and the portable sign was the final stop for the Green Line from

Hertford. It was the long summer evening moving slowly into the night of soft dusty warmth. A few people walked on the pavement. All of them had places they were going to. A policeman asked me if everything was all right.

'I'm waiting for someone,' I told him. I waited with Helena for Ramsden.

In the end, in my desperation, I did write my letter to Ramsden asking her to help me to leave Fairfields, the school where I had gone to live and work taking Helena with me. It was a progressive boarding school. There was not enough food and I was never paid. In my letter I told Ramsden everything that had happened, about my child, about my leaving home, about my loneliness, about my disappointment with the school. I had not expected, I told her, such fraudulent ways. My poverty, I thought, would be evident without any description. After writing the letter I was not able to wait for a reply from Ramsden because, when I went to give notice that I wanted to leave in a fortnight, Patch (the headmistress) replied in her singing voice, the dangerous contralto in which she encouraged people to condemn and entangle themselves, 'By all means but please do go today. There's a bus at the end of the field path at three o'clock.' Neither she nor Miss Myles, after exchanging slightly raised eyebrows with one another, said anything else to me.

I sent my letter to the last address I had from Ramsden almost five years earlier. She was, she said then, still nursing and had a little flat where I would be welcome. Five years is a long time.

I told her in my letter that I would wait for her at the terminus of the Green Line. As I wrote I could not help wondering if she was by now playing the piano in concerts. Perhaps on tour somewhere in the north of England; in the places where concert pianists play. I tried to think of likely towns and villages. As I wrote I wept, remembering Ramsden's kind eyes and her shy manner. Staff nurse Ramsden with her older more experienced face – as someone once described her – and her musician's nose – someone else had said once. She had never known what there was to know about the violin case I carried with me in those days. It had been my intention always to tell her but circumstances changed intentions.

I begged her in the letter and in my heart to be there. Five years is a long time to ignore a kind invitation from someone. A long time to let pass without any kind of reply. With failing hope I walked slowly up and down the pavement which still held the dust and the warmth of the day. I walked and waited with Helena who was white faced and hungry and tired. Sometimes she sat on our heavy case on my roughly folded school winter coat. I tried to comfort myself with little visions of Ramsden playing the piano and nodding and smiling to Helena who would dance, thump-thump, on the carpet in the little living room. I seemed to remember that Ramsden said in the letter, sent all those years ago, that the flat was tiny.

'You'd best be coming along with me.' It was the policeman again. He had passed us several times. Helena was asleep on the folded coat and I was leaning against the railings at the front of an empty house.

The woman in charge of the night shelter gave me a small huckaback towel and a square of green soap. She said she had enough hot water if Helena and I could share the bath.

'She's very like you,' the woman said not trying very hard to hide her curiosity behind a certain sort of kindness. She gave us two slices of bread and butter and a thick cup of tea each. She handed me two grey blankets and said Helena would be able to sleep across the foot of the bed she was able to let me have for one night. The girl who had the bed, she explained, was due to come out of hospital where she had been operated on to have a propelling pencil removed from her bladder.

'The things they'll try,' the woman said. 'I or anyone, for that matter, could have told her she was too far gone for anything like that. All on her own too pore thing. Made herself properly poorly and lorst her baby too.' She looked at Helena who was eating her bread and butter, crusts and all, neatly in what seemed to me to be an excessive show of virtue.

'There's some as keeps their kiddies,' the woman said.

'Yes,' I said avoiding her meaning looks. The night shelter for women carried an implication. There was more than the need of a bed. At St Cuthberts the nurses had not been too sympathetic. I remembered all too clearly herding A.T.S. girls into one of the bathrooms every evening where they sat naked from the waist down in chipped enamel basins of hot water and bicarbonate of soda. In her lectures the Sister Tutor reminded often for the need to let patients be as dignified as possible. The hot basins defied this. Many of the girls were pregnant. Some women, the Sister Tutor said, mistook the orifices in their own bodies. All this, at that time, belonged to other people.

Later my own child was to be the embodiment of all that was poetical and beautiful and wished for. Before she was born I called her Beatrice. I forgot about the A.T.S.

Grateful for the hot bath and the tea and the promised bed I addressed the woman in charge as Sister.

Did the Sister, I asked her, ever know a staff nurse called Ramsden? The woman, narrowing her eyes, thought for a moment and said yes she thought she had – now she recalled it. There was a Ramsden she thought, yes she was sure, who joined the Queens Nurses and went to Mombassa. I tried to take comfort from the doubtful recollection. Yes, went to Mombassa with the Queens Nurses. Very fine women the Queens Nurses. And one night, so she'd heard, the cook in the nurses' quarters was stabbed by an intruder. Horribly stabbed, a dozen or more times in the chest, the neck and the stomach. Apparently the murder was justified, brought on by the cook's own behaviour – him having gone raving mad earlier that same day. But of Ramsden herself she had no actual news.

I understood as I lay under the thin blanket that she had been trying to offer some sort of reply to my stupid and hopeless question. Perhaps the cook in Mombassa was often murdered horribly in these attempts to provide answers.

I tried to sleep but Helena, accustomed to a bed to herself, kicked unbearably all night.

Being at a bus stop, not waiting for a bus, and with the dusk turning quickly to darkness, I think of my father's moon. This moon, once his moon and now mine, is now climbing the warm night sky. It hangs in the branches of a single tree left between the new buildings.

The journey to school is always, it seems, at dusk. My father comes to the first stop. This first journey is in the autumn when the afternoons are dark before four o'clock. The melancholy railway crawls through water-logged meadows where mourning willow trees follow the winding steams. Cattle, knee deep in damp grass, raise their heads as if in an understanding of sorrow as the slow train passes. The roads at the level crossings are deserted. No one waits to wave and curtains of drab colours are pulled across the dimly lit cottage windows.

At the first stop there is a kind of forced gaiety in the meetings on the platform. Some girls have already been to school and others, like me, are going for the first time. My father watches and when the carriage doors are slammed, one after the other, he melts away from the side of the train as it moves slowly along the platform gradually gathering speed, resuming its journey.

I sink back at once into that incredible pool of loneliness which is, I know now but did not understand then, a part of being one of a crowd. I try to think of the moon. Though it is not Easter, my father said before the doors had all slammed, there will be, if the clouds disperse, a moon. He pointed as he spoke towards the dome of the railway station. Because he pointed with his umbrella I felt embarrassed and, instead of looking up, I stared at my shoes. I try to think about his moon being behind the clouds even if I cannot see it. I wish, I am wishing I had smiled and waved to him.

In the noisy compartment everyone is talking and laughing. We are all reflected in the windows and the dark, shadowed fields slip by on both sides.

The school bus, emblazoned with an uplifting motto, rattles through an unfamiliar land. The others sing songs which I have never heard before. There is no moon. The front door of the school opens directly on to the village street. Everyone rushes from the bus and the headmaster and his wife stand side by side in a square of light to receive us.

'Wrong hand Veronica. It is Veronica isn't it?' he ticks my name on a list he has. 'Other hand Veronica. We always shake hands with the right hand.'

When I unpack my overnight bag I am comforted by the new things, the new nightdress, the handkerchiefs and the stockings folded carefully by my mother. Especially my new fountain pen pleases me.

Almost at once I begin my game of comparisons, placing myself above someone if more favourable and below others if less favourable in appearance. This game of appearance is a game of chance. Chance can be swayed by effort, that is one of the rules, but effort has to be more persistent than is humanly possible. It is a game of measuring the unfamiliar against the familiar. I prefer the familiar. I like to know my way, my place with other people, perhaps because of other uncertainties.

I am still on the bench at the bus stop. My father's moon is huge and is now above the tree in a dark-blue space between the buildings. A few cars have come. I have seen their headlights dip and turn off and I have seen the dark shapes of people making their way into the place where my clinic is. They will sit in the comfortable chairs in the waiting room till they are called in to see me. Unavoidably I am late sometimes but they wait.

At the other place where I work there is a scent of hot pines.

The sun, beating down on a nearby plantation all day, brings into the warm still air a heart-lifting fragrance. There is a narrow path pressed into the dry grass and the fallen pine needles. This is the path I take to and from the railway station. Sometimes I suggest to other people that they walk on this path. The crows circling and calling suggest great distance. Endless paddocks with waving crops could be quite close on the other side of the new tall buildings. The corridors indoors smell of toast, of coffee and of hot curries. It is as if there are people cooking at turning points on the paths and in corners between the buildings. It is as if they have casually thrown their saris over the cooking pots to protect them from the prevailing winds.

From where I sit it seems as if the moon is shining with some secret wisdom. I read somewhere that it was said of Chekhov that he *shows us life's depths at the very moment when he seems to reflect its shimmering surface.*

My father's moon is like this.

But the game. The game of comparisons. Before meals at school we have to stand in line beginning with the smallest and ending with the tallest. The room is not very big and the tallest stand over the smallest. We are not allowed to speak and our shoes and table napkins are examined by the prefects. It is during this time of silence and inspection that I make my comparisons. Carefully I am comparing my defects with those of my immediate neighbours. I glance sideways at the pleats of their tunics and notice that the girl next to me bulges. In my mind I call her Bulge; her pleats do not lie flat, they bulge. She is tall and awkward, taller than I am and more round shouldered. I try to straighten my back and to smooth my tunic pleats. I can be better than Bulge. She has cracked lips and she bites her nails. I try not to chew my nails but my hands are not well kept as are the hands of the girl on the other side of me. She has pretty nails and her hair is soft and fluffy. My hair is straight but not as greasy and uneven as Bulge's. Fluffy Hair's feet turn out when she walks. My feet are straight but my stockings are hopelessly wrinkled and hers are not. We all have spots. Bulge's spots are the worst, Fluffy Hair's complexion is the best. She is marred by a slight squint. We all wear spectacles. These are all the same except that Bulge has cracked one of her lenses. My lenses need cleaning.

It is the sound of someone closing a case very quietly in the dormitory after the lights have been turned off which makes me cry. It is the kind of sound which belongs to my mother. This quiet little closing of a case. My nightdress, which she made, is very comfortable. It wraps round me. She knitted it on a circular needle, a kind of stockinette she said it was, very soft, she said. When she had finished it she was very pleased because it had no seams. She was telling our neighbour, showing her the nightdress and the new clothes for school, all marked with my name embroidered on linen tape. The cabin trunk bought specially and labelled clearly 'Luggage in Advance' in readiness for the journey by goods train produced an uneasy excitement. My mother, handling the nightdress again, spoke to me:

ein weiches reines Kleid für dich zu weben,
darin nicht einmal die geringste Spur
Von Naht dich drückt ...

'Shut up,' I said, not liking her to speak to me in German in front of the woman from next door. 'Shut up,' I said again, knowing from the way she spoke it was a part of a poem. 'Shut up,' I crushed the nightdress back into the overnight bag, 'it's only a nightgown!'

When I stop crying I pretend that the nightdress is my mother holding me.

On our second Sunday afternoon I am invited with Bulge and

Fluffy Hair and Helen Ferguson and another girl called Amy to explore a place called Harpers Hill. Bulge is particularly shapeless in her Sunday dress. My dress, we have to wear navy-blue serge dresses, is already too tight for me and it is only the second Sunday. Fluffy Hair's dress belongs to her Auntie and has a red lace collar instead of the compulsory white linen one. The collars are supposed to be detachable so that they can be washed.

I wish I could be small and neat and pretty like Amy, or even quick like Helen Ferguson who always knows what's for breakfast the night before. Very quickly she understands the system and knows in advance the times of things, the difference between Morning Meeting and Evening Meeting and where we are supposed to be at certain times, whose turn it is to mop the dormitory and which nights are bath nights. I do not have this quality of knowing and when I look at Helen Ferguson I wonder why I am made as I am. In class Helen Ferguson has a special way of sitting with one foot slightly in front of the other and she sucks her pen while she is thinking. I try to sit as she does and try to look as if I am thinking while I suck the rounded end of my new pen.

During Morning Meeting I am worrying about the invitation which seems sinister in some way. It is more like a command from the senior girls. I try and listen to the prayer at the beginning of Meeting. We all have to ask God to be in our hearts. All the time I am thinking of the crossroads where we are supposed to meet for the walk. Bulge does not stop chewing her nails and her fingers all through Meeting. I examine my nails, chew them and, remembering, sit on my hands.

Between autumn-berried hedges in unscratched shoes and new stockings we wait at the crossroads. The brown ploughed fields slope to a near horizon of heavy cloud. There are some farm buildings quite close but no sign of people. The distant throbbing of an invisible tractor and the melancholy cawing of the rooks bring back the sadness and the extraordinary fear of the first Sunday afternoon walk too vividly. I try not to scream as I screamed that day and I try not to think about the longed for streets crowded with people and endlessly noisy with trams. It is empty in the country and our raincoats are too long.

The girl, the straw-coloured one they call Etty, comes along the road towards us. She says it's to be a picnic and the others are waiting with the food not far away. She says to follow her. A pleasant surprise, the picnic. She leads us along a little path across some fields to a thicket. We have to bend down to follow the path as it winds between blackberry and under other prickly bushes. Our excited talk is soon silenced as we struggle through a hopeless tangle of thorns and bramble. Amy says she thinks we should turn back. Bulge has the most awful scratches on her forehead. Amy says, 'Look, her head's bleeding.' But Etty says no we shall soon get through to the place.

Suddenly we emerge high up on the edge of a sandy cliff. 'It's a landslide!' I say and, frightened, I try to move away from the edge. Before we have time to turn back the girls, who have been hiding, rush out and grab us by the arms and legs. They tie us up with our own scarves and raincoat belts and push us over the edge and down the steep rough walls of the quarry. I am too frightened to cry out or to resist. Bulge fights and screams in a strange voice quite unlike any voice I have ever heard. Four big girls have her by the arms and legs. They pull her knickers off as she rolls over kicking. Her lumpy white thighs show above the tops of her brown woollen stockings.

'Not this man but Barrabas! Not this man but Barrabas!' they shout. 'She's got pockets in her knickers! Pockets in her knickers!' The horrible chant is all round Bulge as she lies howling.

As quickly as the big girls appeared they are gone. We, none of us, try to do anything to help Bulge as we struggle free from the knotted belts and scarves. Helen Ferguson and Amy lead the way back as we try to find the road. Though we examine, exclaiming, our torn clothes and show each other our scratches and bruises the real hurt is something we cannot speak about.

Fluffy Hair cries. Bulge, who has stopped crying, lumbers along with her head down. Amy, who does not cry, is very red. She declares she will report the incident. 'That's a bit too daring,' I say, hoping that she will do as she says. I am wondering if Bulge is still without her knickers.

'There's Etty and some of them,' Helen Ferguson says as we approach the crossroads. It has started to rain. Huddled against the rain we walk slowly on towards them.

'Hurry up you lot!' Etty calls in ringing tones. 'We're getting wet.' She indicates the girls sheltering under the red-berried hawthorn.

'I suppose you know,' Etty says, 'Harpers Hill is absolutely out of bounds. So you'd better not tell. If you get the whole school gated it'll be the worse for you!' She rejoins the others who stand watching us as we walk by.

'That was only a rag. We were only ragging you,' Etty calls, 'so mind you don't get the whole school gated!' Glistening water drops fly from the wet hedge as the girls leap out, one after the other, across the soaked grass of the ditch. They race ahead screaming with laughter. Their laughter continues long after they are out of sight.

In Evening Meeting Bulge cannot stop crying and she has no handkerchief. Helen Ferguson, sitting next to me on the other side, nudges me and grins, making grimaces of disgust, nodding in the direction of Bulge and we both shake with simulated mirth, making, at the same time, a pretence of trying to suppress it. Without any sound Bulge draws breath and weeps, her eyes and nose running into her thick fingers. I lean away from her heaving body. I can see her grazed knees because both her stockings have huge holes in them.

Before Meeting, while we were in line while two seniors were practising Bach, a duet on the common-room piano, Bulge turned up the hem of her Sunday dress to show me a large three-cornered tear. It is a hedge tear she told me then while the hammered Bach fell about our ears. And it will be impossible, when it is mended, she said, for her mother to lengthen the dress.

I give another hardly visible but exaggerated shiver of mirth and pretend, as Helen Ferguson is doing, to look serious and attentive as if being thoughtful and as if listening with under-standing to the reading. The seniors read in turn, a different one every Sunday. It is Etty's turn to read. She reads in a clear voice. She has been practising her reading for some days.

'Romans chapter nine, verse twenty-one.' Her Sunday dress is well pressed and the white collar sparkles round her pretty neck.

Hath not the potter power
over the clay, of the same lump
to make one vessel unto honour
and another unto dishonour?

'And from verse twenty.' Etty looks up smiling and lisping just a little,

Shall the thing formed say to
him that formed it, Why hast
thou made me thus?

Etty minces from the platform where the staff sit in a semi-circle. She walks demurely back to her seat.

'These two verses,' Miss Vanburgh gets up and puts both hands on the lectern, it is her turn to give the Address, 'These two verses,' she says, 'are sometimes run together.'

'Shall the clay say to the potter why hast thou made me thus ...'

Bulge is still weeping.

Miss Besser, on tiptoe across the creaking boards of the platform, creeps down, bending double between the rows of chairs and, leaning over, whispers to me to take Muriel.

'Take your friend out of Meeting, take her to ...'

'I don't know her. She isn't my friend,' I begin to say in a whisper, trying to explain, 'she's not my friend ...'

'To Matron,' Miss Besser says in a low voice, 'take Muriel.'

I get up and go out with Bulge who falls over her own feet and, kicking the chair legs, makes a noise which draws attention to our attempted silent movement.

I know it is the custom for the one who leads the other to put an arm of care and protection round the shoulders of distress. I know this already after two weeks. It is not because I do not know ...

I wait with Bulge in the little porch outside Matron's cottage. Bulge does not look at me with her face, only with her round and shaking shoulders.

Matron, when she comes, gives Bulge a handkerchief and reaches for the iodine. 'A hot bath,' she says to Bulge, 'and early bed. I'll have some hot milk sent up. Be quick,' Matron adds, 'and don't use up too much hot water. Hot milk,' she says, 'in half an hour.'

I do not go back into Meeting. Instead I stand for a time in a place where nobody comes, between the cloakroom and the bootroom. It is a sort of passage which does not lead anywhere. I think of Bulge lying back if only for a few minutes in the lovely hot water. I feel cold. Half an hour, that is the time Matron has allowed Bulge. Perhaps, if I am quick ...

The lights are out in our dormitory. I am nice and warm. In spite of the quick and secret bath (it is not my night), and the glass of hot milk – because of my bed being nearer the door the maid brings it to me by mistake – (it has been sweetened generously with honey) in spite of all this I keep longing for the cherishing words familiar in childhood. Because of the terrible hedge tear in the navy-blue hem and, because of the lumpy shoulders, I crouch under my bedclothes unable to stop seeing the shoulders without an arm round them. I am not able to weep as Bulge weeps. My tears will not come to wash away, for me, her shoulders.

At night we always hear the seniors, Etty in particular, singing in the bathroom. Two of them, tonight, may have to miss their baths. Etty's voice is especially noticeable this night.

little man you're crying, she sings,
little man you're blue
I know why you're crying
I know why you're blue
Some-one stole your Kiddi-Kar away from you

The moon, my father's moon, is too far away.

RECHA

The constant sound of television might be for a great many people what a mountain stream was to Wordsworth. Instead of these I have the sound of doves.

There are times during these golden afternoons when I know that I am not hearing the doves. It seems impossible that I should not hear them when they sidle to and fro, back and forth, along the edge of the roof above my window, endlessly scraping and tapping and rustling along the tremulous gutters. If I do hear them it is only because I hear them all the time, even when they are not there. Their voices are like the voices of a family, heard still even though this family has ceased to exist.

The little guest, on heat, I remember quite clearly, all those years ago, replete with more than food, stuffed, they would say now, took away with her my silk frock and the Swiss cotton embroidered pillow-slips with which my mother, to honour and please a visitor rather than to offer mere shelter to a homeless refugee, had made the bed.

She, the little guest, tipping forward on high heels, walks to and fro on the kitchen floor busily scraping left-over morsels of food on to saucers. Scraps of fried bread and bits of chopped-up liver. She carries them one by one to the pantry shelf. As she walks

41

she lets slip from her person little swabs of bloodstained cotton wool. These catch on her heels and are trodden, back and forth, mottling the tiles as if with squashed strawberries.

'It is as if she is on heat,' my mother says.

'The expression, this expression,' my father corrects gently, 'is not, as a rule in English, applied to a human being.'

'Bloodstain,' my mother complains, 'everywhere a bloodstain. Look! Wherever she goes. People, when they grow up, should be able to look after themselves. They should be able to look after their *monatsfluss*.'

Later my mother comes to me.

'Lend Recha your dress, the new one,' she says, persuading. 'Lend her the new dress, the one with the little blue flowers.'

'The one with the forget-me-not flowers? But it's my Liberty silk. It's my good dress. I haven't worn it yet.'

'Yes. Yes. I know but Recha has an interview. She has to go for an interview. You know, she might find for herself a post as a housekeeper. She has no home now. She must find herself a home. We must help her.'

'But she's not my size. The skirt will be much too long.'

'I know this. We can gather it up at the waist. You understand. With a nice sash. You have some ribbon ...'

'Why hasn't she got a home then? A house. She's here now in England. She's got a husband. An English soldier, isn't he? He was here with her, in my room, in my bed. Why can't she go? With him? She's safe now.'

'He is in a camp,' my mother explains. 'I don't need to tell you. She has to find somewhere to live. He has had to go back to Salisbury, to his camp.'

'But he must have a family, her mother-in-law why can't she ...?'

'Be quiet now,' my mother says quickly, 'she is coming downstairs again.'

Recha stands in front of the long mirror in my mother's bedroom twitching the soft folds of my dress over her plump body. She pulls at her black hair frizzing it out on her forehead.

Her cheeks are red and shine as if about to burst.

'Senk you,' she says to me. I have never seen her before. She is already, with her husband, in my room when I come home from school for the summer holiday. My sister tells me straight away that there are people in my room. It is her room too. She has a bed in our mother's room. She tells me that for ages now people have been arriving, sometimes on the night train from London, arriving and going to bed at once, sleeping and sleeping and then talking in whispers and crying.

'The crying is the worst,' she says. She says she heard one woman crying all night. Even our father was not able to stop her crying.

'He walks to the station in the night,' my sister says. She says that he has given away his winter coat and that it's all right for now but what will he do in winter.

'These people,' my mother says, 'they have nothing. Recha must have packed the things in her luggage with her rags and bits of cotton wool.' She explains the treachery in her soft up-and-down voice. 'Perhaps she thought they were gifts from us.' Her voice is like a stream running. 'The time!' she says to my father, 'it's time for you to leave for the station. Look!' she says, 'Look at the time!'

Two more people are arriving. They will have our bedroom. My sister and I move our bedclothes once more.

'The oil-cloth on here is so thin the horsehair's prickling through,' I complain to my sister.

'I'll have the sofa then,' she says. 'I'll sleep there.'

'Oh no. It's all right.' We slide off the sofa laughing as we did when we were little. One of our old games.

I am ashamed because I have been robbed. This is the strange thing about it. When one is robbed there is this feeling of being ashamed. I do not want to admit to anyone that my silk frock has been stolen. And, even more, I do not want my father and mother to admit that they have been deceived in any way. Especially by people they are trying to help, and in their own house.

But of course they do not even think they have been deceived or robbed.

'Recha,' my mother is saying to my father in the kitchen, 'Recha has never done any housework or cooking in her life. How will she manage as housekeeper? She has such beautiful hands.'

Simply, my mother and father are seeing impossible suffering, especially people being separated from each other or making hurried marriages in order to escape from something they are not able to endure, something they must, at all costs, get away from.

'It is an irony, is it called irony?' My mother's soft voice reaches the horsehair sofa. She is talking still to my father. 'Is it called irony? If it was once a joke,' she says, 'for a bespectacled shrimp of an intellectual, a Jew, to be an officer in a Red Cossack regiment during the Polish campaign of 1920, is this the same joke, if it can be called a joke, which is being repeated now twenty years later?' I have heard her before talking about these men, the grey beards, she calls them, with their gold-rimmed glasses and flying side curls, desperate to disguise their accents and their hand movements, marching or trying to march, walking on thin bent legs, their narrow shoulders and their intellectual superiority, 'bowing,' she is saying it again, 'to the healthy pink flesh of the English Tommies.'

My father's voice, like a boulder in a wild mountain stream, interrupts her. I can hear his deep voice soothing.

It is not like my mother to use a word like Tommy. If English people use it they say Our Tommies, Our Boys, not English Tommies. I pull my sheets back over the inadequate horsehair. I think, in the morning, I will correct my mother so that she need not make a mistake of this sort in front of the neighbours.

BATHROOM DANCE

When I try on one of the nurse's caps my friend Helen nearly dies.

'Oh!' she cries, 'take it off! I'll die! Oh if you could see yourself. Oh!' she screams and Miss Besser looks at me with six years of reproach stored in the look.

We are all sewing Helen's uniform in the Domestic Science room. Three pin-striped dresses with long sleeves, buttoned from the wrist to the elbow, double tucks and innumerable button holes; fourteen white aprons and fourteen little caps which have to be rubbed along the seam with a wet toothbrush before the tapes can be drawn up to make those neat little pleats at the back. Helen looks so sweet in hers. I can't help wishing, when I see myself in the cap, that I am not going to do nursing after all.

Helen ordered her material before persuading me to go to the hospital with her. So, when I order mine it is too late to have my uniform made by the class. It is the end of term, the end of our last year at school. My material is sent home.

Mister Jackson tells us, in the last Sunday evening meeting, that he wants the deepest responsibility for standards and judgements in his pupils, especially those who are about to leave the happy family which is how he likes to think of his school. We must not, he says, believe in doing just what we please. We must always believe in the nourishment of the inner life and in the loving discipline of personal relationships. We must always be concerned with the relentless search for truth at whatever cost to tradition and externals. I leave school carrying his inspiration and his cosiness with me. For some reason I keep thinking about and remembering something about the reed bending and surviving and the sturdy oak blown down.

My mother says the stuff is pillow ticking. She feels there is nothing refined about nursing. The arrival of the striped material has upset her. She says she has other things in mind for me, travelling on the continent, Europe, she says, studying art and ancient buildings and music.

'But there's a war on,' I say.

'Oh well, after the war.'

She can see my mind is made up and she is sad and cross for some days. The parcel, with one corner torn open, lies in the hall. She is comforted by the arrival of a letter from the Matron saying that all probationer nurses are required to bring warm sensible knickers. She feels the Matron must be a very nice person after all and she has my uniform made for me in a shop and pays extra to have it done quickly.

Helen's mother invites me to spend a few days with Helen before we go to St Cuthberts.

The tiny rooms in Helen's home are full of sunshine. There are bright-yellow curtains gently fluttering at the open windows. The garden is full of summer flowers, roses and lupins and delphiniums, light blue and dark blue. The front of the house is covered with a trellis of flowers, some kind of wisteria which is sweetly fragrant at dusk.

Helen's mother is small and quiet and kind. She is anxious and always concerned. She puts laxatives in the puddings she makes.

I like Helen's house and garden, it is peaceful there and I would like to be there all the time but Helen wants to do other things. She is terribly in love with someone called David. Everything is David these few days. We spend a great deal of time outside a milkbar on the corner near David's house or walking endlessly in the streets where he is likely to go. No one, except me, knows of this great love. Because I am a visitor in the house I try to be agreeable. And I try to make an effort to understand intense looks from Helen, mysterious frowns, raised eyebrows, head shakings or noddings and flustered alterations about arrangements as well as I can.

'I can't think what is the matter with Helen,' Mrs Ferguson says softly one evening when Helen rushes from the room to answer the telephone in case it should be David. We are putting up the black-out screens which Mrs Ferguson has made skilfully to go behind the cheerful yellow curtains every night. 'I suppose she is excited about her career,' she says in her quiet voice, picking up a little table which was in Helen's way.

Everyone is so keen on careers for us. Mister Jackson, at school, was always reading aloud from letters sent by old boys and girls who are having careers, poultry farming, running boys' clubs and digging with the unemployed. He liked the envelopes to match the paper, he said, and sometimes he held up both for us all to see.

Helen is desperate to see David before we leave. We go to all the services at his mother's church and to her Bible class where she makes us hand round plates of rock cakes to the Old Folk between the lantern slides. But there is no David. Helen writes him a postcard with a silly passionate message. During the night she cries and cries and says it is awful being so madly in love and will I pretend I have sent the postcard. Of course I say I won't. Helen begs me, she keeps on begging, saying that she lives in the neighbourhood and everyone knows her and will talk about her. She starts to howl and I am afraid Mrs Ferguson will hear and, in the end, I tell her, 'All right, if you really want me to.'

In the morning I write another card saying that I am sorry about the stupid card which I have sent and I show it to Helen, saying, 'We'll need to wash our hair before we go.'

'I'll go up first,' she says. While she is in the bathroom using up all the hot water, I add a few words to my postcard, a silly passionate message, and I put Helen's name on it because of being tired and confused with the bad night we had. I go out and post it before she comes down with her hair all done up in a towel, the way she always does.

Mrs Ferguson comes up to London with us when we set off for St Cuthberts. Helen has to dash back to the house twice, once for her camera and the second time for her raincoat. I wait with Mrs Ferguson on the corner and she points out to me the window in the County Hospital where her husband died the year before. Her blue eyes are the saddest eyes I have ever seen. I say I am sorry about Mr Ferguson's death, but because of the uneasiness of the journey and the place where we are going, I know that I am not really concerned about her sorrow. Ashamed, I turn away from her.

Helen comes rushing up the hill, she has slammed the front door, she says, forgetting that she put the key on the kitchen table and will her mother manage to climb through the pantry window in the dark and whatever are we waiting for when we have only a few minutes to get to the train.

David, unseen, goes about his unseen life in the narrow suburb of little streets and houses. Helen seems to forget him easily, straight away.

Just as we are sitting down to lunch there is an air-raid warning. It is terrible to have to leave the plates of food which have been placed in front of us. Mrs Ferguson has some paper bags in her handbag.

'Mother!' You can't!' Helen's face is red and angry. Mrs Ferguson, ignoring her, slides the salads and the bread and butter into the bags. We have to stand for two hours in the air-raid shelter. It is very noisy the A.R.P. wardens say and they will not let us leave. It is too crowded for us to eat in there and, in any case, you can't eat when you are frightened.

Later, in the next train, we have to stand all the way because the whole train is filled with the army. Big bodies, big rosy faces, thick rough greatcoats, kitbags, boots and cigarette smoke wherever we look. We stand swaying in the corridor pressed and squeezed by people passing, still looking for somewhere to sit. We can't eat there either. We throw the sad bags, beetroot soaked, out onto the railway lines.

I feel sick as soon as we go into the main hall at St Cuthberts. It is the hospital smell and the smell of the bread and butter we try to eat in the nurses' dining room. Helen tries to pour two cups of tea but the tea is all gone. The teapot has a bitter smell of emptiness.

Upstairs in Helen's room on the Peace corridor as it is called because it is over the chapel, we put on our uniforms and she screams with laughter at the sight of me in my cap.

'Oh, you look just like you did at school,' she can't stop laughing. How can she laugh like this when we are so late. For wartime security the railway station names have been removed and, though we were counting the stops, we made a mistake and went past our station and had to wait for a bus which would bring us back.

'Lend me a safety pin,' I say, 'one of my buttons has broken in half.' Helen, with a mouthful of hair grips, busy with her own cap, shakes her head. I go back along the corridor to my own room. It is melancholy in there, dark, because a piece of black-out material has been pinned over the window and is only partly looped up. The afternoon sun of autumn is sad too when I peer out of the bit of window and see the long slanting shadows lying across unfamiliar fields and roads leading to unknown places.

My school trunk, in my room before me, is a kind of betrayal. When I open it books and shoes and clothes spill out. Some of my pressed wildflowers have come unstuck and I put them back between the pages remembering the sweet, wet grass near the school where we searched for flowers. I seem to see clearly shining long fingers pulling stalks and holding bunches. Saxafrage, campion, vetch, ragged robin, star of Bethlehem, wild strawberry and sorrel. Quickly I tidy the flowers – violet, buttercup, King cup, cowslip, coltsfoot, wood anemone, shepherd's purse, lady's slipper, jack in the pulpit and bryony ...

'No Christian names on duty please,' staff nurse Sharpe says, so, after six years in the same dormitory, Helen and I make a great effort. Ferguson – Wright, Wright – Ferguson.

'Have you finished with the floor mop – Ferguson?'

'Oh, you have it first – Wright.'

'Oh! No! by all means, after you Ferguson.'

'No, after you Wright.'

Staff nurse Sharpe turns her eyes up to the ceiling so that only the whites show. She puts her watch on the window sill saying, 'Quarter of an hour to get those baths, basins and toilets really clean and the floors done too. So hurry!'

'No Christian names on duty,' we remind each other.

We never sleep in our rooms on the Peace corridor. Every night we have to carry out blankets down to the basement where we sleep on straw mattresses. It is supposed to be safe there in air raids. There is no air and the water pipes make noises all night. As soon as I am able to fall asleep Night Sister Bean is banging with the end of her torch saying, 'Five-thirty a.m. nurses, five-thirty a.m.' And it is time to take up our blankets and carry them back upstairs to our rooms.

I am working with Helen in the children's ward. Because half the hospital is full of soldiers the ward is very crowded. There are sixty children; there is always someone laughing and someone crying. I am too slow. My sleeves are always rolled up when they should be rolled down and buttoned into the cuffs. When my sleeves are down and buttoned it seems they have to be rolled up again at once. I can never remember the names of the children and what they have wrong with them.

The weeks go by and I play my secret game of comparisons as I played it at school. On the Peace corridor are some very pretty nurses. They are always washing each other's hair and hanging their delicate underclothes to dry in the bathroom. In the scented steamy atmosphere I can't help comparing their clothes with mine and their faces and bodies with mine. Every time I am always worse than they are and they all look so much more attractive in their uniforms, especially the cap suits them well. Even their finger nails are better than mine.

'Nurse Wright!' Night Sister Bean calls my name at breakfast.

'Yes Sister.' I stand up as I have seen the others do.

'Matron's office nine a.m.' she says and goes on calling the register.

I am worried about my appointment with the Matron. Something must be wrong.

'What did Matron want?' Ferguson is waiting for me when I go to the ward to fetch my gas mask and my helmet. I am anxious not to lose these as I am responsible for them and will have to give them back if I leave the hospital or if the war should come to an end.

'What did Matron want?' Ferguson repeats her question, giving me time to think.

'Oh it is nothing much,' I reply.

'Oh come on! What did she want you for? Are you in trouble?' she asks hopefully.

'Oh no, it's nothing much at all.' I wave my gas mask. 'If you must know she wanted to tell me that she is very pleased with my work and she'll be very surprised if I don't win the gold medal.' Ferguson stares at me, her mouth wide open, while I collect my clean aprons. She does not notice that one of them is hers. It will give me an extra one for the week. I go to the office to tell the ward sister that I have been transferred to the theatre.

Had I the heavens' embroidered cloths,
    Enwrought with golden and silver light,

O'Connor, the theatre staff nurse, is singing. She has an Irish accent and a mellow voice. I would like to tell her I know this poem too.

The blue and the dim and the dark cloths
Of night and light and the half light,

In the theatre they are all intimate. They have well-bred voices and ways of speaking. They look healthy and well poised and behave with the ease of movement and gesture which comes from years of good breeding. They are a little circle in which I am not included. I do not try to be. I wish every day, though, that I could be a part of their reference and their joke.

In a fog of the incomprehensible and the obscure I strive, more stupid than I have ever been in my life, to anticipate the needs of the theatre sister whose small, hard eyes glitter at me above her white cotton mask. I rush off for the jaconet.

'Why didn't you look at the table!' I piece together her angry masked hiss as I stand offering a carefully opened and held sterilized drum. One frightened glance at the operating table tells me it is catgut she asked for.

'Boil up the trolley,' the careless instruction in the soft Irish voice floats towards me at the end of the long morning. Everything is on the instrument trolley.

'Why ever didn't you put the doctors' soap back on the sink first!' The theatre is awash with boiled-over soap suds. Staff nurse O'Connor, lazily amused, is just scornful enough. 'And,' she says, 'what in God's Holy Name is this!' She fishes from the sterilizer a doll-sized jumper. She holds it up in the long-handled forceps. 'I see trouble ahead,' she warns, 'better not let sister see this.' It is the chief surgeon's real Jaeger woollen vest. He wears it to operate. He has only two and is very particular about them. I have discovered already that sister is afraid of the chief surgeon, consequently I need to be afraid of her. The smell of boiled soap and wool is terrible and it takes me the whole afternoon to clear up.

Theatre sister and staff nurse O'Connor, always in masks, exchange glances of immediate understanding. They, when not in masks, have loud voices and laugh. They talk a great deal about horses and dogs and about Mummy and Daddy. They are quite shameless in all this Mummy and Daddy talk.

The X-ray staff are even more well-bred. They never wear uniform and they sing and laugh and come into the theatre in whatever they happen to be wearing – backless dinner dresses, tennis shorts or their night gowns. All the time they have a sleepy desirable look of mingled charm and efficiency. War-time shortages of chocolate and other food stuffs and restrictions on movement, not going up to London at night for instance, do not seem to affect them. They are always called by pet names, Diamond and Snorter. Diamond is the pretty one, she has a mop of curls and little white teeth in a tiny rosebud mouth. Snorter is horsey. She wears trousers and little yellow waist coats. She always has a cigarette dangling from her bottom lip.

I can't compare myself with these people at all. They never speak to me except to ask me to fetch something. Even Mr Potter, the anaesthetist who seems kind and has a fatherly voice, never looks in my direction. He says, holding out his syringe, 'Evipan' or 'Pentothal', and talks to the others. Something about his voice, every day, reminds me of a quality in my father's voice; it makes me wish to be back at home. There is something hopeless in being hopeful that one person can actually match and replace another. It is not possible.

Sometimes Mr Potter tells a joke to the others and I do not know whether I should join in the laugh or not.

I like Snorter's clothes and wish that I had some like them. I possess a three-quarter-length oatmeal coat with padded shoulders and gilt buttons which my mother thinks is elegant and useful as it will go with everything. It is so ugly it does not matter what I wear it with. The blue skirt I have is too long, the material is heavy, it sags and makes me tired.

'Not with brown shoes!' Ferguson shakes her head.

It is my day off and I am in her room. The emptiness of the lonely day stretches ahead of me. It is true that the blue skirt and the brown shoes, they are all I have, do look terrible together.

Ferguson and her new friend, Carson, are going out to meet some soldiers to go on something called a pub crawl. Ferguson,

I know, has never had anything stronger than ginger beer to drink in her life. I am watching her get ready. She has frizzed her hair all across her baby round forehead. I can't help admiring her, the blaze of lipstick alters her completely.

Carson comes in balancing on very high-heeled shoes. She has on a halo hat with a cheeky little veil and some bright-pink silk stockings.

'What lovely pink stockings!' I say to please her.

'Salmon, please,' Carson says haughtily. Her hair is curled too and she is plastered all over with ornaments, brooches, necklaces, rings and lipstick, a different colour from Ferguson's. Ferguson looks bare and chubby and schoolgirlish next to Carson.

Both of them are about to go when I suddenly feel I can't face the whole day alone.

'It's my day off too,' I say, 'and I don't know where to go.'

Ferguson pauses in the doorway.

'Well, why don't you come with us,' Carson says. Both of them look at me.

'The trouble is, Wright,' Carson says kindly, 'the trouble is that you've got no sex appeal.'

After they have gone I sit in Ferguson's room for a long time staring at myself in her mirror to see if it shows badly that I have no sex appeal.

I dream my name is Chevalier and I search for my name on the typed lists on the green baize notice boards. The examination results are out. I search for my name in the middle of the names and only find it later at the top.

My name, not the Chevalier of the dream, but my own name is at the top of the lists when they appear.

I work hard in all my free time at the lecture notes and at the essays 'Ward Routine', 'Nursing as a Career', 'Some Aspects of the History of Nursing' and 'The Nurse and her Patient'.

The one on ward routine pleases me most. As I write the

essay, the staff and the patients and the wards of St Cuthberts seem to unfold about me and I begin to understand what I am trying to do in this hospital. I rewrite the essay collecting the complete working of a hospital ward into two sheets of paper. When it is read aloud to the other nurses, Ferguson stares at me and does not take her eyes off me all through the nursing lecture which follows.

I learn every bone and muscle in the body and all the muscle attachments and all the systems of the body. I begin to understand the destruction of disease and the construction of cure. I find I can use phrases suddenly in speech or on paper which give a correct answer. Formulae for digestion or respiration or for the action of drugs. Words and phrases like gaseous interchange and internal combustion roll from my pen and the name at the top of the lists continues to be mine.

'Don't tell me you'll be top in invalid cookery too!' Ferguson says and she reminds me of the white sauce I made at school which was said to have blocked up the drains for two days. She goes on to remind me how my pastry board, put up at the window to dry, was the one which fell on the headmaster's wife while she was weeding in the garden below, breaking her glasses and altering the shape of her nose forever.

My invalid carrot is the prettiest of them all. The examiner gives me the highest mark.

'But it's not even cooked properly!' Ferguson is outraged when she tastes it afterwards. She says the sauce is disgusting.

'Oh well you can't expect the examiner to actually eat all the things she is marking,' I say.

Ferguson has indigestion, she is very uncomfortable all evening because, in the greedy big taste, she has nearly the whole carrot.

It is the custom, apparently, at St Cuthberts to move the nurses from one corridor to another. I am given a larger room in a corridor called Industry. It is over the kitchens and is noisy and smells of burning saucepans. This room has a big tall window. I move my bed under the window and, dressed in my school jersey, I lie on the bed for as long as possible to feel the fresh cold air on my face before going down to the basement for the night. Some evenings I fall into a deep and refreshing sleep obediently waking up, when called, to go down to the doubtful safety below.

Every day, after the operations, I go round the theatre with a pail of hot soapy water cleaning everything. There is an orderly peacefulness in the quiet white tranquillity which seems, every afternoon, to follow the strained, bloodstained mornings.

In my new room I copy out my lecture notes:

... infection follows the line of least resistance ...

and read my school poetry book:

Through the thick corn the scarlet poppies peep,
And round green roots and yellowing stalks I see
Pale pink convolvulus in tendrils creep;
And air-swept lindens yield
Their scent ...

I am not able to put out of my mind the eyes of a man who is asleep but unable to close his eyes. The putrid smell of wounded flesh comes with me to my room and I hear, all the time, the sounds of bone surgery and the troubled respiration which accompanies the lengthy periods of deep anaesthetic ...

Oft thou hast given them store
Of flowers – the frail leaf'd, white anemony,
Dark blue bells drench'd with dews of summer eves
And purple orchises with spotted leaves ...

... in the theatre recovery ward there are fifteen amputations, seven above the knee and eight below. The beds are made in two halves so that the padded stumps can be watched. Every bed has its own bell and tourniquet ...

St Cuthberts is only a drop in the ocean; staff nurse O'Connor did not address the remark to me, I overheard it.

Next to my room is a large room which has been converted into a bathroom. The dividing wall is a wooden partition. The water pipes make a lot of noise and people like to sing there, usually something from an opera.

One night I wake from my evening-stolen sleep hearing two voices talking in the bathroom. It is dark in my room; I can see some light from the bathroom through a knot-hole high up in the partition. The voices belong to Diamond and Snorter. This is strange because they live somewhere outside the hospital and would not need to use that bathroom. It is not a comfortable place at all, very cold, with a big old bath awkwardly in the middle of the rough floor.

Diamond and Snorter are singing and making a lot of noise, laughing and shrieking above the rushing water.

Singing:

Give me thy hand O Fairest
 la la la la la la la
I would and yet I would not

laughter and the huge bath obviously being filled to the brim.

Our lives would be all pleasure

 tra la la la la la la
 tra la la la la la la

 tum pe te tum

 tum pe te tum

'That was some party was it not!'
'Rather!' Their rich voices richer over the water.
I stand up on my bed and peer through the hole which is

about the size of an egg. I have never looked through before, though have heard lots of baths and songs. I have never heard Diamond and Snorter in there before – if it is them.

It is Diamond and Snorter and they are naturally quite naked. There is nothing unusual about their bodies. Their clothes, party clothes, are all in little heaps on the floor. They, the women not the clothes, are holding hands, their arms held up gracefully. They are stepping up towards each other and away again. They have stopped singing and are nodding and smiling and turning to the left and to the right, and, then, with sedate little steps, skipping slowly round and round. It is a dance, a little dance for two people, a minuet, graceful, strange and remote. In the steam the naked bodies are like a pair of sea birds engaged in mating display. They appear and disappear as if seen through a white sea mist on some far off shore.

The dance quickens. It is more serious. Each pulls the other more fiercely, letting go suddenly, laughing and then not laughing. Dancing still, now serious now amusing. To and fro, together, back and forth and together and round and round they skip and dance. Then, all at once, they drop hands and clasp each other close, as if in a private ballroom, and quick step a foxtrot all round the bathroom.

It is not an ugly dance, it is rhythmic and ridiculous. Their thighs and buttocks shake and tremble and Snorter's hair has come undone and is hanging about her large red ears in wispy strands.

The dance over, they climb into the deep hot bath and tenderly wash each other.

The little dance, the bathroom dance, gives me an entirely new outlook. I can't wait to see Diamond and Snorter again. I look at everyone at breakfast, not Ferguson, of course (I know everything there is to know about her life) with a fresh interest.

Later I am standing beside the patient in the anaesthetic room, waiting for Mr Potter, when Snorter comes struggling through the swing doors with her old cricket bag. She flops about the room dragging the bag:

she says, as she always does, while rummaging in the bag for her white wellington boots. I want to tell Snorter, though I never do, that I too know this poem.

I look hard at Snorter. Even now her hair is not combed properly. Her theatre gown has no tapes at the back so that it hangs, untied and crooked. She only has one boot on when Mr Potter comes. The unfairness of it all comes over me. Why do I have to be neatly and completely dressed at all times. Why do they not speak to me except to ask for something to be fetched or taken away. Suddenly I say to Snorter, '*Minuet du Salle de la Bain*', in my appalling accent. I am surprised at myself. She is hopping on one foot, a wellington boot in her hand, she stops hopping for a moment.

'*de la salle de bain surely*,' she corrects me with a perfect pronunciation and a well-mannered smile. 'Also lower case,' she says, 'not caps, alters the emphasis.'

'Oh yes of course,' I mutter hastily. An apology.

'Pentothal.' Mr Potter is perched on his stool at the patient's head, his syringe held out vaguely in my direction.

NIGHT RUNNER

Night Sister Percy is dying. It is my first night as Night Runner at St Cuthberts. Night Sister Bean, grumbling and cackling, calls the register and, at the end, she calls my name.

'Nurse Wright.'

'Yes Sister,' I reply, half rising in my chair as I have seen the others do. The Maids' Dining Room, where we eat, is too cramped to do anything else.

'Night Runner,' she says and I sit down again. The thought of being Night Runner is alarming. Nurse Dixon has been Night Runner for a long time. All along I have been hoping that I would escape from these duties and responsibilities, the efficient rushing here and there to relieve on different wards; every night bringing something new and difficult.

The Night Runner has to prepare the night nurses' meal too; one little sitting at twelve midnight and a second one at twelve forty-five and, of course, the clearing up and the washing up.

Every night I admire Nurse Dixon in the tiny cramped kitchen where we sit close together, regardless of rank, in the hot smell of warmed up fish or mince and the noise of the jugs of strong black coffee, keeping hot, in two black pans of boiling water. We eat our meal there in this intimacy with these two hot saucepans splashing and hissing just behind us. The coffee, only a little at the bottom of each jug, looks thick and dark and

I wonder how it is made. Tonight I will have to find out and have it ready when the first little group of nurses appears.

When I report to Night Sister Bean in her office, she tells me to go for the oxygen.

'Go up to Isolation for the oxygen,' she says without looking up from something she is writing. I am standing in front of her desk. I have never been so close to her before, not in this position, that is, of looking at her from above. She is starch scented, shrouded mysteriously in the daintily severe folds of spotted white gauze. She is a sorceress disguised in the heavenly blue of the Madonna; a shrivelled, rustling, aromatic, knowledgeable, Madonna-coloured magician; she is a wardress and a keeper. She is an angel in charge of life and in charge of death. Her fine white cap, balancing, nodding, a grotesque blossom flowering for ever in the dark halls of the night, hovers beneath me. She is said to have powers, an enchantment, beyond the powers of an ordinary human. For one thing, she has been on night duty in this hospital for over thirty years. As I stand there I realize that I do not know her at all and that I am afraid of her.

'Well,' she says, 'don't just stand there. Go up to Isolation for the oxygen and bring it at once to Industry.'

'Yes, Sister,' I say and I go as quickly as I can. The parts of the hospital are all known by different names; Big Boys Big Girls, Top Ward, Bottom Ward, Side Ward and Middle, Industry, Peace, Chapel and Nursery. I have a room on the Peace corridor, so named because it is above the chapel and next to Matron's Wing.

Industry is the part over the kitchens. There are rooms for nurses there too. Quite often there is a pleasant noise and smell of cooking in these rooms. The Nurses' sick bay is there and it is there that I have to take the oxygen.

I am frightened out here.

For one thing, Isolation is never used. It is, as the name

suggests, isolated. It is approached by a long, narrow covered way sloping up through a war-troubled shrubbery where all the dust bins are kept. Because of not being able to show any lights it is absolutely dark there. When I go out into the darkness I can smell rotting arms and legs, thrown out of the operating theatre and not put properly into the bins. I gather my apron close so that I will not get caught by a protruding maimed hand.

When I flash my torch quickly over the bins I see they are clean and innocent and have their lids firmly pressed on. In the torchlight there is no smell.

The sky at the end of the covered passage is decorated with the pale moving fans of search lights. The beams of light are interwoven with the sounds of throbbing engines. The air-raid warning might sound at any moment. In the emergency of being made Night Runner so suddenly, I have forgotten to bring my tin hat and gas mask from the Maids' Dining Room.

I am worried about the gas mask and the tin hat. I have signed for them on arrival at the hospital and am completely responsible for them. I will have to hand them back if I leave the hospital or if this war comes to an end. Usually I never leave either of them out of my care. I have them tied together with thick string. I put them under my chair at meal times and I hang them up in the nurses' cupboard on the ward where I am working.

It is hard to find the oxygen. My torch light picks up stacks of pillows, shelves of grey blankets, rolls of waterproof sheets, and some biscuit tins labelled Emergency Dressings, all with dates on them. There are two tea chests filled with tins and bottles. The chests are marked Emergency, Iron Rations, Doctors Only in red paint. There do not seem to be similar boxes marked for nurses or patients.

At last I find the oxygen cylinder and I rush with the little trolley up to Industry.

Sister Percy is dying. She is the other Night Sister and is very fat. She is propped, gasping, on pillows, a blue trout with eyes bulging, behind the floral screens made by Matron's mother for sick nurses.

It is the first time I have seen someone who is dying. Night Sister Bean is there and the R.M.O. and the Home Sister. They take the oxygen and Sister Bean tells me I need not stay. She pulls the screens closer round Sister Percy.

In the basement of the hospital I set about the secrets of making the coffee and having it come only so far up the jugs.

Later Night Sister Bean comes and says why haven't I lit the gas, which, when you think about it, is a good thing to say as they will surely want that potato and mince stuff hot. Before she leaves she makes me get down on my knees to hunt behind the pipes for cockroaches. She has a steel knitting needle for this and we knock and scrape and rattle about, Night Sister Bean on her knees too, and we chase them out, the revolting things, and sprinkle some white powder which, she says, they love to eat without knowing it is absolutely fatal to them.

It is something special about night duty, this little meal time in the middle of the night, with everyone sitting together, even Night Sister Bean, herself, coming to one or the other of the sittings. She seems almost human, in spite of the mysterious things whispered about her, at these meals. Sometimes she even complains about the sameness of them, saying that one thing the war cannot do is to make these meals worse than they are and that it is sheer drudgery to eat them night after night. When I think about this I realize she has been eating stewed mince and pounded fish for so many years and I can't help wishing I could do something about it.

This first night it takes me a long time to clear up in the little pantry. When at last I am finished Night Sister Bean sends me to relieve on Bottom Ward. There is a spinal operation in the theatre recovery room just now, she says, and a spare nurse will be needed when the patient comes back to the ward.

On my way to Bottom Ward I wish I could be working with staff nurse Ramsden.

'I will play something for you,' she said to me once when I was alone and filled with tears in the bleak, unused room which is the nurses' sitting room.

She ran her fingers up and down the piano keys. 'This is Mussorgsky,' she said. 'It's called Gopak, a kind of little dance,' she explained. She played and turned her head towards me nodding and smiling. 'Do you like this?' she asked, her eyes smiling. It is not everyone who has had Mussorgsky played for them; the thought gives me courage as I hurry along the unlit passage to the ward.

There is a circle of light from the uncurtained windows of the office in the middle of the ward. I can see a devout head bent over the desk in the office. I feel I am looking at an Angel of mercy who is sitting quietly there ready to minister to the helpless patients.

Staff nurse Sharpe is seated in the office with an army blanket tucked discreetly over her petticoat. Her uniform dress lies across her lap. She explains that she is just taking up the hem and will I go to the kitchen and cut the bread and butter. As I pass the linen cupboard I see the other night nurse curled up in a heap of blankets. She is asleep. This is my friend Ferguson.

I sink slowly into the bread cutting. It is a quiet and leisurely task. While I cut and spread I eat a lot of the soft new bread and I wonder how Sharpe will manage to wear her uniform shortened. Matron is so particular that we wear them long, ten inches off the ground, so that the soldiers do not get in a heightened excitement about us.

Sharpe comes in quite soon. She seems annoyed that I have not finished. She puts her watch on the table and says the whole lot, breakfast trays all polished and set, and bread and butter for sixty men, must be finished in a quarter of an hour. I really hurry up after this and am just ready when the operation case comes back and I have to go and sit by him in the small ward. I hope to see Ferguson but staff nurse Sharpe has sent her round changing the water jugs.

Easily I slip into my dream of Ferguson. She owes me six and sevenpence. I have written it on the back of my writing pad. I'll go out with her and borrow two and six.

'Oh Lord!' I'll say, 'it's my mother's birthday and I haven't a thing for her and here I am without my purse. Say, can you lend me two and six?' And then I'll let her buy a coffee and a bun for me that will bring it to three shillings and I won't ever pay it back and, in that way, will recover some of the six and sevenpence.

'Cross my heart, cut me in two if my word is not true,' I say to myself and I resolve to sit in Ferguson's room as soon as I am off duty. I'll sit there till she pays me the money. I'll just sit and sit there till it dawns on her why I am there.

The patient, quite still as if dead, suddenly moves and helps himself to a drink of water. He vomits and flings the bowl across the room. He seems to be coming round from his anaesthetic. I grope under the bedclothes. I should count his pulse but I am unable to find his wrist.

'Oh I can't,' he groans, 'not now I can't.'

He seems to be in plaster of paris from head to foot. He groans again and sleeps. Nervously I wait to try again to find some place on his body where I can feel his pulse.

High on the wall in the Maids' Dining Room is an ancient wireless. It splutters and gargles all day with the tinny music of workers' play time and Vera Lynn plaintively announcing there'll always be an England. Sometimes in the early mornings, while we have our dinner, the music is of a different kind. Sometimes it is majestic, lofty and sustaining.

'Wright!' Staff nurse Ramsden calls across the crowded tables. 'Mock Morris? Would you say?' She waves a long-fingered hand.

'No,' I shake my head, 'not Mock Morris, it's Beethoven.' She laughs. She knows it is not Beethoven. It is a little joke we have come to share. It is the only joke I have with anyone. Perhaps it is the same for Ramsden. She has a slight moustache and I have noticed, in her room, an odour, a heaviness which belongs with older women perhaps from the perfumed soap she has and the material of well-made underwear. Her shoes and stockings, her suits and blouses and hats have the fragrance of being of a better quality. Ramsden asked me once about the violin I was carrying. She has said to me to choose one of her books, she has several in her room, as a present from her to me. Secretly I think, every day, that I admire Ramsden. I love her. Perhaps. I think, I will tell her, one day, the truth about the violin case.

A special quality about working during the night is the stepping out of doors in the mornings, the first feeling of the fresh air and the sun which is hardly warm in its brightness.

We ride our bicycles. Not Ramsden. There is a towing patch along the river. I, not knowing it before, like the smell of the river, the muddy banks and the cattle-trodden grass. Water birds, disturbed, rise noisily. Our own voices echo.

Though we have had our meal we want breakfast. Ferguson hasn't any money. Neither has Queen. Ferguson says she will owe Queen if Queen will owe me for them both. We agree and I pay. And all the way back I am trying to work out what has to be added to the outstanding six and sevenpence.

Ferguson's room, when I go to sit there, looks as if it should be roped off as a bomb crater. Her clothes, and some of mine, are scattered everywhere. There is a note from the Home Sister on her dusty dressing table. I read the note, it is to tell Ferguson to clean her hair brush.

Bored and sleepy I study the note repeatedly, and add 'Neither a Borrower nor a Lender be' in handwriting so like the Home Sister's it takes my breath away.

I search for Ferguson's writing paper. It is of superior quality and very suitable. I write some little notes in this newly learned handwriting and put them carefully in my pocket. I continue to wait for Ferguson, hardly able to keep my eyes open.

I might have missed my sleep altogether if I had not remembered in time that Ferguson has gone home for her nights off.

I do not flash the torch for fear of being seen. I grope in the dark fishing for something, anything, in the cavernous tea chest, and hasten back down the covered way.

Night Sister Bean says to me to go to Bottom Ward to relieve and I say, 'Yes Sister', and leave her office backwards, shuffling my feet and bending as if bowing slightly, my hands, behind my back, clasping and almost dropping an enormous glass jar.

It is bottled Chinese gooseberries, of all things, and I put one on each of the baked apples splashing the spicy syrup generously. Night Sister Bean smiles, crackling starch, and says the baked apples have a piquant flavour. She has not had such a delicious baked apple for thirty years. 'Piquant!' she says.

Staff nurse Sharpe sits in the office all night with nursing auxiliary Queen. Queen has put operation stockings over her shoes to keep warm. Both Sharpe and Queen are wrapped up in army blankets. Sharpe has to let down the hem of her dress. Sister Bean asked her to stay behind at breakfast.

Whenever I come back to the office Sharpe says, 'Take these pills to bed twelve' or 'Get the lavatories cleaned,' and, 'Time to do the bread and butter – and don't leave the trays smeary like last night.'

At the end of the ward I pull out the laundry baskets and I move the empty oxygen cylinders and the fire equipment; the buckets of water and sand. I simply move them all out from their normal places, just a little way out, and later, when Sharpe and Queen go along to the lavatory, they fall over these things and knock into each other, making the biggest disturbance ever heard in a hospital at night. Night Sister Bean comes rushing all the way up from her office in the main hall. She is furious and tells Sharpe and Queen to report to Matron at nine a.m.

She can see that I am busy, quietly with my little torch, up the other end of the ward, pouring the fragrant mouth wash in readiness for the morning.

The tomato sauce has endless possibilities. The dressed crab is in such a small quantity that the only thing I can do is to put a tiny spoonful on top of the helpings of mashed potato. Night Sister Bean is appreciative and says the flavour seeps right through. Tinned bilberries, celery soup and custard powder come readily to my experienced hands.

I do not see staff nurse Ramsden very often. She has not asked me in to her room again to choose the book. Perhaps she has changed her mind. She is, after all, senior to me.

There are times when an unutterable loneliness is the only company in the cold early morning. The bicycle rides across the heath or along the river are over too quickly and, because of this, are meaningless. With a sense of inexplicable bereavement my free time seems to stretch ahead in emptiness. I go to bed too soon and sleep badly.

I am glad when Ferguson comes back; very pleased. In the pantry I am opening a big tin, the biggest thing I have managed to lift out so far. I say 'Hallo' to Ferguson as she sits down with the other nurses; they talk and laugh together. I go on with my work.

'Oh, you've got IT,' I say to Ferguson. 'Plenty of S.A. Know what that is? Sex appeal, it's written all over you.' And seeing, out of the corner of my eye, Night Sister Bean coming in, I go on talking as if I haven't seen her.

'How you do it beats me Fergie,' I say. 'How is it you have all the men talking about you the way they do? You certainly must have given them plenty to think about. They all adore you. Corporal Smith's absolutely mad about you, really!' Unconcernedly I scrape scrape at the tin. 'He never slept last night. Sharpe had to slip him a Mickey Finn, just a quick one.

He's waiting for another letter from you and I think he's sending the poem you asked for. Who on earth is your go between?' So I go on and scrape scrape at the tin.

I know why there is silence behind me. I turn round.

'Oh, here you are at last Sister,' I say to Night Sister Bean. Ferguson is a dull red colour, pity, as she was looking so well after her nights off.

'Here we are Sister,' I say, 'on the menu we have Pheasant Wing in Aspic. Will you have the fish pie with it?' I serve all the plates in turn. The coffee hisses and spits behind us.

'Matron's office, nine o'clock,' Night Sister Bean says to Ferguson.

'Yes, Sister.'

Ferguson is sent to Big Girls for the rest of the night and I am to relieve, as usual, on Bottom Ward. I wake Corporal Smith at four a.m. and urge him to write to Nurse Ferguson. 'Every day she waits for a letter,' I tell him, 'she'll get ill from not eating if you don't write.' Staff nurse Sharpe finds me by his bed and sends me to scrub the bathroom walls.

'And do out all the cupboards too, and quickly,' she says.

In the morning when I see Sharpe safely in the queue for letters I rush up to the Peace corridor and find her room. I cram her curtains into her messy wet soap dish and leave one of my neatly folded notes on her dressing table.

Do not let your curtains dangle in the soap dish. Sister.

There is not much I can do with cherry jam. I serve it with the stewed mince as a sweet and sour sauce. It is a favourite with the Royal family, I tell them, but I can see I shall have to risk another raid on my secret store.

The next night I have a good dig into both chests and load myself up with tinned tomato soup, a tinned chicken, some sardines and two tins of pears.

Nurse Dixon is mystified. Her eyes are full of questions.

'Where d'you get all ...' her lips form whispered words.

'No time to chat now, sorry,' I say. I am hastily setting a little tray for Night Sister Bean. I have started taking an extra cup of coffee along to her office. It seems the best way to use up a tin of shortbread fingers. Balancing my tray I race up the dark stairs and along the passage to Night Sister Bean's office.

'Bottom Ward,' Night Sister Bean says without looking up. Again I am at the mercy of Sharpe.

'Wash down the kitchen walls,' she says, 'and do all the shelves and cupboards and quickly – before you start the blanket baths.' She gives me a list of the more disagreeable men to do; she says to change their bottom sheets too. All the hardest work while nursing auxiliary Queen, who is back there, and herself sit wrapped up in the office, smoking, with a pot of hot coffee between them on the desk.

I go into the small ward and give the emergency bell there three rings bringing Night Sister Bean to the ward before Sharpe and Queen realise what is happening.

'Is it an air raid?' Queen asks anxiously.

'Nurses should know why they ring, Nurse,' Sister Bean says and she makes them take her round to every bed whispering the diagnosis and treatment of every patient. Night Sister Bean rustling and croaking, fidgetting and cursing, disturbs all the men trying to find out who rang three times.

'Someone must be haemorrhaging,' she says, 'find out who it is.'

Peering maliciously into the kitchen, Sister Bean sees me quietly up the step ladder with my little pail of soapy water. The wet walls gleam primrose yellow as if they have been freshly painted. She tells Sharpe and Queen to report to Matron's office nine a.m. for smoking on duty.

Once again Sharpe is in the letter queue. I take the loaded ash tray from the Porters' Lodge and spill it all over her room.

Your room is disgusting. Take some hot water and disinfectant and wash down Sister

The folded note lies neatly on her dressing table.

I try listening to Beethoven but it reminds me of my loneliness. I wish Corporal Smith would write to me. I wish someone would write to me. Ferguson is going to The Old Green Room for coffee. She is popular, always going out.

In my room I have a list.

1. Listen to Beethoven.
2. Keep window wide open. If cold sleep in school jersey.
3. Ride bicycle for complexion. (care of)
4. Write and Think.

'I can't come out,' I say to Ferguson. 'I'm listening to Beethoven,' I say, ignoring the fact that she has not asked me.

'It's only one record,' she says, 'you've only got one record.'

'It's Beethoven all the same.' I beat time delicately and wear my far away look.

Ferguson goes off out and I add number 5 with difficulty to the list. The paper is stuck in at the side of the dressing-table mirror and uneven to write on.

5. Divide N.S.B.'s nature and discover exactly the extent of her powers.

I take my white windsor, bath size, to the wash room and fill a basin with hot water to soften the soap. I set to work with my nail file and scissors. I'll take my torch tonight, I'm thinking, a tin of powdered milk would be useful. Whipped up, it makes very good cream; delicious with the baked apples.

The likeness is surprising. It is the distinction of the shape and the tilt of the cap, the little figure is emerging perfectly. I work patiently for a long time. I am going to split the image in half very carefully and torture one half keeping the other half as a control, as in a scientific experiment, and observe the effect on the living person.

The idea is so tremendous I feel faint. Already I foresee results, the upright, crisp little blue and white Bean totters in the passage, she wilts and calls for help.

'Nurse Wright! Help me up, dear. What a good child you are, so gentle too. Just help me to that chair, thank you, dear child. Thank you!'

The Peace corridor is very quiet. Another good thing about the night duty is that we all may sleep in our beds during the day. Every morning I long for this sleep. Up until this time, I, like the others, have had to carry bedclothes down to the basement every night because of the air raids. There are no beds in the basement, only some sack mattresses of straw. There is no air there either.

I love the smell of the clean white windsor. I am sculpting carefully with the file. The likeness is indeed perfect. My hands are slippery and wrinkled and I am unable to stop them from shaking. I feel suddenly that I possess some hitherto unknown but vital power to be able to make this – this effigy.

And then, all at once, Night Sister Bean is there in the doorway of the wash room, peering about to see who it is not in bed yet and it is after twelve noon already. Because I am thinking of the moment when I will split the image and considering which tool will be most suitable for this, the sudden appearance of Sister Bean is, to say the least, confusing.

I plunge my head into the basin together with Her I am so carefully fashioning, saying, 'Oh, I can never get the soap out of my hair!', delighted at the sound of weariness achieved.

She says to remember always to have the rinsing water hotter than the washing water. 'Hot as you can bear it,' she says.

'Thank you Sister.'

She is rustling and cackling, crackling and disturbing, checking every corner of the wash room, quickly looking into all the lavatories, saying as she leaves, 'And it is better to take off your cap first.'

So there I am with the soaked limp thing, frothed and scummed all over with the white windsor, on my head, still secure with an iron foundry of hair grips and useless for tonight. My work of art too is ruined, the outlines blurred and destroyed before being finished. It is a solemn moment of understanding that from a remote spot, namely the door, she has been able to spoil what I have made and add a further destruction of her own, my cap.

My back aches with bending over the stupid little sink. These days I am missing too much sleep. In spite of being so tired I go down to the ramp where the milk churns are loaded and unloaded. It is the meeting place of the inside of the hospital with the outside world. The clean laundry boxes are there, neatly stacked. Fortunately Ferguson's box is near the edge. I open it and remove one of her fresh clean caps. My box is there too but I don't want to take one of mine as it will leave me short later in the week.

The powdered household milk is in the chest as I hoped, tins of it and real coffee too. I find more soup, mushroom, cream of asparagus, cream of chicken, vegetable and minestrone. I am quite reckless with my torch. Christmas is coming, I take a little hoard of interesting tins.

I discover that Night Sister Bean has a weakness for hot broth and I try, every night, to slip a cup along to her office in the early part of the night before I start on anything else.

Several things are on my mind, mostly small affairs. For some time I have Corporal Smith's love letter to Ferguson, sixteen pages, in my pocket. It is not sealed and her name does not appear anywhere in the letter. It is too long for one person so I divide the letter in half and address two envelopes in Corporal Smith's handwriting, one to Sharpe and one to Ferguson. Accidentally I drop them, unsealed, one by the desk in Night Sister Bean's office and the other in the little hall outside Matron's room. We are not supposed to be intimate with the male patients and I feel certain too that Corporal Smith is a married man, but there is something else on my mind; it is whether a nurse should send a Christmas card to the Matron. It is something entirely beyond my experience.

In the end I buy one, a big expensive card, a Dutch Interior.

It costs one and ninepence. I sit a whole morning over it trying to think what I should write.

A very Happy Christmas to Matron from Nurse Wright Nurse Wright sounds presumptuous. I haven't taken an external exam yet. She may not regard me as nurse.

A Very Happy Event ... that would be quite wrong.

A very Happy Christmas to You from Guess Who. She might think that silly.

Happy Christmas. Vera. Too familiar. *Veronica* I have never liked my name.

A Happy Christmas to Matron from one of her staff and in very small writing underneath *N/V Wright.*

I keep wondering if all the others will send Matron a Christmas card. It is hardly a thing you can ask anyone. Besides I do not want, particularly, to give Ferguson the idea. She will never think of it herself. And who can I ask if I don't ask her?

I put the card in Matron's correspondence pigeon hole. The card is so big it has to be bent over at the top to fit in. I am nervous in case someone passing will see me.

Again I am relieving on Bottom Ward. Always it is this Bottom Ward. This time I have to creep round cleaning all the bed wheels.

'And quietly,' Sharpe says, 'Nurse Queen and I don't want everyone waking up!'

The card worries me. I will take it out in the morning. The message is all wrong.

One of her staff! I can't bear to think about it.

The card is still there, bending, apologizing and self conscious in the morning. I want to remove it but there are people about and correspondence must not be tampered with.

Twice during the day I get dressed and creep down from the Peace corridor, pale, hollow-eyed and drab; all night nurses are completely out of place in the afternoons. I feel conspicuous, sick nearly, standing about in the hall waiting to be alone there so that I can remove that vulgar card and its silly message. It is still bending there in the narrow compartment.

Even when the hall is free of people there are two nurses chattering together by the main door. Whyever do they stand in this cold place to talk. I have to give up and go back to bed, much too cold to sleep. Ferguson has my hot-water bottle for her toothache. It seems I can never get even with her. Never ever.

The card is still there in the evening when we go down to the Maids' Dining Room for breakfast. I can hardly eat as I am thinking of a plot to retrieve the card.

The register is finished.

'Nurse Wright.'

'Yes Sister?' half rising in my chair as we all do in that cramped place.

'Matron's office nine a.m. tomorrow.'

'Yes Sister,' I sit down again. It can't be to thank me for the card as it hasn't been received yet. A number of reasons come to mind, for one thing there are the two deep caves of dark emptiness; perhaps they have been discovered ...

In spite of a sense of foreboding I go, with my little torch hidden beneath my apron, up the long covered way. I need more powdered milk. The path seems endless. The night sky has the same ominous decoration; throbbing engines alternate with sharp anti-aircraft guns and the air-raid sirens wail up and down, up and down. The soft searchlights move slowly. They make no noise and are helpless. I feel exposed and push my hands round the emptiness of the nearest tea chest. Grabbing a tin of powdered milk I rush back down past the festering bins and on down towards an eternity of the unknown.

I have a corner seat in this train by a mistake which is not entirely my fault. The woman, who is in this seat, asks me if I think she has time to fetch herself a cup of tea. I can see that she badly wants to do this and, in order that she does not have to go without the tea, I agree that, though she will be cutting it fine, there is a chance that she will have time. So she goes and I see her just emerging from the refreshment room with a look on her face which shows how she feels. She has her tea clutched in one hand and I have her reserved seat because it is silly, now that the train has started, to stand in the corridor being crushed by army greatcoats and kitbags and boots, simply looking at the emptiness of this comfortable corner.

I have some household milk for Mother, it is always useful in these days of rationing. I have the tinned chicken also. At the last minute I could not think what to do with it as Night Sister Bean will not be naming the next Night Runner till this evening, and, of course, I shall not be there to know who it is and so am not able to hand on either the milk or the chicken.

There is too the chance that the new Night Runner might be my friend Ferguson. It would not do to give her these advantages.

This is my first holiday from St Cuthberts, my nights off and ten days holiday. Thirteen days off.

'Shall I take my tin hat, I mean my helmet, and my gas mask?' I ask Matron.

'By all means if you would like to,' she says and wishes me a pleasant holiday and a happy Christmas.

The tin hat and the gas mask are tied to my suitcase. My little sister will be interested to see them.

My father will be pleased with his Christmas card. He has always liked the detail and the warm colours of a Dutch Interior. He will not mind the crossing out inside. The card will flatten if I press it tonight in the dictionary.

For some reason I am thinking about staff nurse Ramsden. Last night, in the doorway of the Maids' Dining Room, I stood aside to let her go in first.

'Thank you,' she said and then she asked me what my first name was.

'First name?'

'Yes, your Christian name, what is it?' her voice, usually low, was even lower. Like a kind of shyness.

I did not have the chance to answer. We had to squeeze through to our different tables quickly as Night Sister Bean was already calling the register.

If Ramsden could be on the platform to meet my train at the end of this journey I would be able to answer her question. Perhaps I would be able to explain to her about the violin case. I would like to see Ramsden, I would like to be going to her. Thinking about her and seeing her face, in my mind, when she turned to smile at me, the time when she played Mussorgsky on the piano in the nurses' sitting room, makes me think that it is very probable, though no one has ever spoken about it, that Night Sister Bean might very well be missing her life-long friend Night Sister Percy. Missing her intolerably.

LOIS

This is a piano concerto, Lois. Lois, listen! Listen to the way the piano rushes in. It's the Emperor Concerto, Lois. It's not really hard to listen to, is it? Is it? But Lois, wait. Listen. All the same. Listen to this.

Ashes of Roses, the perfume is called that. No, not perfume really, Lois. It's only scent. Little bottle of scent to take to boarding school. Ashes of Roses to bring to the hospital.

Lois, you'll never believe this. I was so unhappy at boarding school to begin with. My mother put scent on my handkerchief for me to take back and hold when I went to sleep.

Silly but it's real. Lois, you like the scent, do you? You did say you liked the scent. You told me you liked the fragrance. You smell nice, you said that to me once. It's Ashes of Roses. I told you, it's the Ashes of Roses.

Tango Bolero now. Not the Emperor. The Tango. I'm glad you asked to share with me Lois when we had the chance to change.

From this high window the world is out there. The trees. You could paint the trees, Lois. The park is over to the right and on this side there's the railway and the canal. Did you notice this evening, Lois, how the water shines as the rest of the world gets dark? And last week, Lois, did you see that, in the moonlight, the water shines all night? Did you see that? Can't put a black-out curtain over the canal, can you? All those places out there, the buildings, the warehouses and the railway and the dark streets. All dark, in darkness. People inside those houses don't know who can see their upstairs windows and their roof tops.

Tango. Tango Bolero. Lois. Listen! Someone's coming!

'What is that noise? Nurse? Whatever is that terrible noise?'

'It's music, Sister. It's the Tango Bolero.'

'Tango. Fango. Turn it off this instant! I never heard such a noise in all my life. Do you know what time it is?'

'No Sister. Sorry Sister.'

'It's practically midnight! Where is the music? For heavens sake. Where is it coming from?'

'It's in the wardrobe, Sister, I'll turn it off.'

'And Nurse! Where is your nightdress? You've got nothing on! Why haven't you got your nightdress on?'

'I, er, I was too hot Sister.'

'Well child! For heavens sake open the window. And put the black-out back. If you're careful, slip your hand behind the curtain, put a book or something to hold the curtain down.'

'Yes Sister. Thank you Sister.'

'Why aren't you on duty Nurse?'

'We're, I mean, I'm on nights off Sister.'

'I see. Nurse! I never saw, in my life, such an untidy room. Your room is a disgrace and the beds! Is that your pillow? Pull the pillow out and put it back where it belongs. And try to remember that others want and need their sleep. And another thing, Nurse, it is not healthy to sleep without your gown. See that you put it on at once.'

'Yes Sister. Thank you Sister.'

'Has she gone? The old witch?'

'Yes. That was close. Yes, she's gone.'

'I was suffocating under all that heap. Who was it?'

'Home Sister.'

'Yep. I know that. But who? Which witch?'

'Morton.'

'Forget her! Let's put the tango on again. Don't put your nighty on. Here, push the towel in the gramophone and this blanket over the top and close the wardrobe this time.'

'And listen! Let's open the window and take down the black-out so if she comes back she can't switch on the light.'

'Good idea. And put the chair against the door.'

Ashes of Roses. Tango Bolero. Like this. Put your arms round me. Like this. Tango.

Of course at a time like this, I know, it is not right to actually think of anyone, I mean to really think of another person just now. But there is just this, that that witch Morton might be on her way back up here. And if I go on thinking of another person the awful thing is that Sister Bean might be coming up with her.

THE HUNT

The early morning sunlight filters through the bushes outside my window making tremulous patterns of light and shade on the wall opposite. This partly shaded shadow-moving light makes the room serene and tranquil. I try to prolong the tranquillity by keeping my thoughts as peaceful as possible. Sometimes I have a wish to keep on staring into the leaves and the small branches out there until I disappear into them. Once I saw a hand in the leaves. It seemed to be reaching towards me, it was my own hand. I often hold out my hand now towards the bushes in order to see this enticing reflection. I wish too, often in the evenings, for an elixir, an ancient potion with magic qualities. A provider of energy and enlightenment.

Os innominatum Ilium Ischium Acetabulum and *the Symphysis Pubis,* the poetry of anatomy. It's like poetry I want to tell them, this anatomy, this usefulness of the pelvis. We are studying together, in the room I share with Lois, for our exams. *The Ilium presents two surfaces, external and internal, a crest, two processes, anterior and posterior and an articulating surface for the sacrum.* I want to tell them, Trent and Ferguson, that I am going to a house party at Dr Metcalf's. Lois has just come in so I do not say anything. Dr Metcalf gave me the invitation in Magda's purple handwriting this morning on the ward. I have missed the opportunity. I can't tell them now.

'Any cigs?' Lois asks, knowing that none of us smokes and knowing too that I will have a packet of State Express 333 especially for her. State Express is her favourite. Ferguson does not like Lois. Lois does not seem to notice Ferguson.

'The crest of the ilium is curved and surmounts the bone, here it is,' I say quickly, the point of my pencil hovering over the bone on the page. And with the other hand I pull the present for Lois out of my pocket slipping it to her sideways. Trent raises her eyebrows.

'I can read you like a book,' she says to me out of the corner of her mouth. 'Dead Loss,' she says, 'brother to Joe Loss.' She makes me laugh.

I do not say anything about the invitation. I shall be coming in very late. I shall have to sign the book and ask the night porter to unlock for me. I wonder whose name I should sign. Ferguson's or Trent's? If names appear too often in the late pass book it is a question of appearing on Sister Bean's list for Matron's office at nine a.m. I would never use Lois's name. I have some feelings for her which I am not able to define. I feel happy when she comes into the room. Her clothes amuse me. I have a great wish to protect her and to do things for her. I like giving her small presents and seeing her pleasure. I make up my mind, as Lois shrouds us in smoke, to put Helen Ferguson in the book. It is Sunday. It is my day off. I did not go out because of the party tonight and because of the forthcoming exams. I wanted to go on sleeping too, on my bed in this room I have with Lois. We only sleep in the basement now if there is an air-raid warning. There was a prolonged one last night.

The night porter, because it is Sunday, will be a relieving one. He will not know me. I can be H. Ferguson for him.

'Describe the acetabulum,' Trent says, 'and do it without looking at the book.'

'A deep, cup-shaped cavity, formed by the union of three bones ...' Helen Ferguson's voice reminds me of our first days and weeks at the hospital, of the first Sunday here ...

On my first Sunday I had the evening off. I wanted to be on my bed. The bed wasn't even made up. The bedclothes were rolled neatly in readiness for carrying downstairs later on. It was late afternoon towards the end of summer. A narrow shaft of sunshine came through the little space where the black-out curtain was tied up in a loop. It was very quiet and then someone started playing the organ in the chapel below. I liked the music and I tried not to sleep. I wanted to hear the organ but could hardly keep my eyes open. Images, one after the other in that familiar ritual of oncoming sleep, crowded my thoughts. Images from the children's ward, the noise, the big black trays on which we carried little tin plates of mince and potatoes and the baked apples swimming in yellow cream and covered with the shining crystals of brown sugar. 'Good food,' staff nurse Sharpe, who was teaching me, said, 'is essential in their treatment. You must see that every child eats the dinner.' Images from the children's ward, the occupational therapist moving slowly between the beds and the frames like a walking sewing basket. Twice in one morning one of the boys cut her scissors off and she had to find a new piece of string. Staff nurse Sharpe explained that she kept the scissors tied to her overall. She seemed, with her white hair, to be elderly but Sharpe said no it was because all her family were killed when their house was bombed and her hair had gone white overnight. In all the noise of shouting and crying and dropping tin plates or cups and the boys throwing conkers, the therapist played the piano in the middle of the ward and some of the little ones, rolling their heads from side to side, sang.

The good ship sails on the anny anny O
The anny anny O
The good ship sails on the anny anny O ...

We have stopped studying for a few minutes as Trent is making some toast and cocoa in the little kitchen at the end of the passage. Lois says have I still got some cake left.

The children in the ward, when they sing, can only roll their heads from side to side because of being strapped on to their frames. Mrs Doe, the wardsmaid who is unable to read and write, crashes the tin plates, Sharpe says they are aluminium, into the sink. I envy Mrs Doe. She says she goes to the pictures with her old man Fridays. I envy her because she can go home at night. She cleans the floors and washes up and comes and goes through a back door. She says exactly what she thinks about us. She calls it giving us a piece of her mind.

And all the time while the work is being done, all through the terrible noise and rush, Vera Lynn is singing on the wireless. She sings 'There'll always be an England' and something that sounds like 'There'll be blue birds over the white cliffs of Dover'. I like the therapist but we have no reason to talk to each other and I don't know her name or where she lives.

It seemed to me during the first few days that there was a smell of disease, of tuberculosis and when I asked staff nurse Sharpe about this, in a moment when she seemed approachable, she said no the disease did not smell. She thought it was the little woollen shawls the children all had, they probably needed washing and it was something I could get done on the first fine day.

When I lay on my bed that first Sunday evening someone came along the Peace corridor knocking on all the doors, opening them and closing them. Tap tap of heels on the floorboards, knock knock open door click close door click all the way along.

Now it is my door. I keep my eyes closed. I hope whoever it is will go away. It is my first Sunday in this place and I am tired. I have never been so tired. My hands and arms up to the elbows are all chapped and sore. My feet hurt. I would leave if I knew how to.

'Time for chapel Nurse!' It is Sister Bean. Why isn't she in bed? She is the Night Sister. 'Time for chapel Nurse!' as if she is wound up for these words. She closes the door and I hear her tap tap knock knock to the end of Peace and back tap knock open click close click all along the other side. And then tap tap back to my door knock open click.

'Time for chapel Nurse!'

'I am a Quaker, Sister.'

'Time for chapel Nurse!'

In candlelight and incense and the music of the organ Father Bailey, the portly one, and Father Reynold who is hungry and red-nosed pass, in their robes, to and fro, up and down the aisles between the rows of pretty nurses. All have on fresh clean caps and aprons. All, with devout expressions, are bending their heads down, repeating *I believe*. It is called the creed. I have never heard it before. At the door I was given an unfamiliar little book. It is nicely bound in leather and the pages are edged with gold. I would like to keep it. There is a squat tuffet thing for me to kneel on. We kneel and sit and kneel and stand and sit and when we all move there is a rustling like leaves falling in autumn. There is a chanting and a murmuring of believing. I am not sure what I believe and, unless I read in the little book (if I can find the page), I do not know the words. At school prayers were silent in our own words in our hearts. I see two nurses, two of the ones I have been working with, they are very pious.

On their dressing tables they both have silver-framed photographs and every day their conversations, in well-bred voices, ripple across the Peace corridor.

'Oh Mandy Darling, have you heard from Derek lately?'

'Yes Darling, simply adorable letter this morning.'

'How heavenly Darling! I adore his big ears.'

'Barrington Darling have *you* heard from Rojji Rogère?'

'Mm yes Darling, this morning. He's on a Brenn Gun Carrier.'

'Oh Wizard!'

It is Nurse Mandy who holds the crying children, the little boys, over the jet of icy water in the sluice room every morning to punish them for wetting their cots. They go on crying and crying, their voices hoarse from crying. She is saying this '*I believe*,' she believes in a whole list of things and I am trying to keep my eyes open ...

'What's in the *acetabular fossa*?' Ferguson's question – it's her turn after answering correctly – is for me.

'Fat,' I say. They laugh but it is correct.

'What and where,' it is my turn to ask Trent, 'what and where is the *ligamentum teres*?'

It is not possible to compare, to make comparisons, between this room which is Dr Metcalf's and any of my mother's rooms. On the ground floor she has the back room and the front room and the kitchen. In this house, which is the Metcalf's house, I cannot begin to know how many rooms there are, parts of the house are unknown to me. All the same I am making comparisons. Dr Metcalf has a carpet; at home we have linoleum and a rug, a black rug in case the coal spits and burns. There are some books at home, here the walls are lined with books. This room is Dr Metcalf's study. It is not very light, there is a shaded reading lamp. The electric light at home hangs in the middle of the room on a flex from the ceiling. My father likes bright light.

'Don't read with a bad light,' he is always saying it, 'you'll spoil your pretty eyes. Don't spoil your pretty eyes.'

This is a much bigger house, a better house, there are more

rooms than we have at home. Perhaps I should have gone home instead of coming here. It is a whole week since the party. Dr Metcalf had to leave in the middle of it as he was wanted at the hospital. I wanted to leave then to go with him but Magda would not hear of it.

'Precious child stay!' she cried all across the room. 'You simply can't go yet. I'll pop you in a taxi.' And then she asked me to come the next free evening I had because she was going to be away, 'and Jonty must, simply must have some good company,' she said. 'He wants to play some music called *The Hunt*,' she said. I told her I'd like that very much and all the guests thought this very funny.

'Oh! isn't she just a pet,' Magda cried then. 'Come here precious pet!' She told me she wanted to hug me and kiss me forever.

On the way to the Metcalf's this evening I keep hoping that Dr Metcalf will answer the door. I do not like Mrs Privett, the housekeeper. I think I am afraid of her. Magda calls her Mrs P. Really it is more that Mrs P dislikes me. Magda encourages Mrs P in her disapproval of everything because, she says, when Mrs P is hating she works terribly hard and polishes everything and scours the saucepans, haven't I noticed how shiny they are.

Mrs P does let me in and she opens the door only a little way so that I have to step in sideways.

'Dr Metcalf is expecting me,' I say, my voice all silly and shaky with nervousness. It seems a long time that I am waiting for him to come and I worry in case he does not really want me to come or that he has forgotten that I am coming. I try to work out how much in pounds, shillings and pence his curtains and chair covers will have cost. I look up and down the walls and the books and at the furnishings adding value and subtracting.

Dr Metcalf, when he comes in, is very nice and gently helps me off with my coat. He winds up the gramophone and puts on the record. But there is something wrong with it. We can hardly hear it. I feel I should say it is nice but we both know something is wrong. He stops the gramophone and takes off the record. He explains it is a quartet by Mozart, it's called *The Hunt*. He says he is sorry it's a flop and I say it doesn't matter. There is a silence between us which I feel I must fill.

I kneel down and look along the book cases hoping to recognize a title and make some intelligent remark but all the books are strange to me. I read aloud some of the titles. Dr Metcalf looks amused.

'Which would you like to read?' he asks after a little silence. I tell him that I'm afraid I don't know. He bends down and takes a book.

'Try this one,' he says, and kneels beside me.

My clumsy skirt is caught all round my legs as I struggle awkwardly to my feet. The book is *The Voyage Out* by someone called Virginia Woolf.

'A lady writer,' I say and feel ashamed to have said such a stupid thing. 'Thank you,' I say. I like his hand, the feeling of it, as he gives me the book. I tell him I am afraid it might be too difficult for me.

'Try it,' he says getting up. He says he thinks Mrs P is going out but she has left us some supper and, if I like, we can have it by the fire in his study. Would I like that, he wants to know.

'Yes,' I say, glad that Mrs P is going out, 'that would be nice.'

A patient has given Dr Metcalf some rhubarb. He shows it to me in the kitchen and I offer to cook it for him. He sits on the edge of the table while I wash it and cut it up. I try to do this neatly and not to strip it too much. It needs a lot of sugar I tell him. It is a moment of authority which I enjoy. But when we look for the sugar there isn't any. Mrs P must have had it all in her tea he says and I wish I had brought my ration with me but of course I didn't know about the rhubarb.

The kitchen is transformed, that's how Dr Metcalf puts it, by the fragrance of the stewed rhubarb. He will eat it, he says, for breakfast. He carries our supper through to the study.

We do not eat much. I am shy sitting there with a tray between us. I hardly notice what there is to eat. Some sort of salad with pears in it. I feel I have said silly things about his books. Because he is quiet I talk, feeling all the time that I am talking too much.

'I suppose it's about six miles, I go there on my bike, I like the ride, it's country there, hawthorn berries and rose hips on both sides of the road, the wild roses when they are out are so pretty. Her house is in the middle of a field. Hens, she keeps hens.' I am telling Dr Metcalf about Gertrude's Place. 'I could,' I tell him, 'bring some eggs, one time, for Magda, perhaps next time,' I say, 'I go there on my days off but if I don't go Mother goes on the bus.'

Dr Metcalf is always quiet, I suppose, it does not show, this quietness, so much when Magda and the others are there. In one of the silences we hear Mrs P returning. Dr Metcalf says she has come back earlier than usual. In another of the silences I say that I am thinking it is time for me to go back to the hospital. When I say this Dr Metcalf says he will take me back. And I say oh no I would not dream of him coming out again. He says a walk would be nice. He feels like a walk. Should we walk to the hospital? Or do I prefer to go by bus?

'Oh a walk would be lovely,' I say.

Outside the front door, to our surprise, there is a thick fog. It is impossible to see even one footstep ahead. It is as if a cold damp wall is right up against us. Slowly we go forward. I feel along the wall with both hands. We can follow the wall I say but Dr Metcalf reminds me that the wall does not go beyond the corner of the street. We come to the end of the wall. I feel completely enveloped. My scarf, coat and gloves are wet. I try to go back. I reach for the wall but am not able to find it. I can't breathe. I stumble off the unseen edge of the pavement. There is a silence so terrible it is as if the world has ceased to exist. I feel terrified and try to call out to Dr Metcalf and find he is near me. He puts his arm round me and says it is no good, we'll have to find our way back to the house and it will be best for me to sleep there and go in to the hospital in the morning.

Mrs Privett has already gone to bed but Dr Metcalf taps on her door and asks if I can sleep in her sitting room. He explains about the fog and that we have had to leave our wet things in the kitchen. He brings a mattress from one of the spare beds upstairs and puts it on her sitting-room floor. Mrs P, who looks more sour than usual in her dressing gown and curlers, hands me two sheets. Dr Metcalf brings down an armful of blankets. He says goodnight to Mrs P and me in a most formal way. I can hardly bear this and I want to drop the sheets and rush along the passage and into the hall and up the big staircase after him. I want to be upstairs in his part of the house, even though he is alone up there. I don't want to be an unwelcome guest in Mrs Privett's sitting room.

'Can I have a glass of water please,' I ask Mrs P. She brings me half a glass which she holds out to me round the door before closing it. I make up a sort of bed on the floor.

Mrs Privett's sitting room is crowded with her things. There is only just room for the mattress between the chairs and the table and the sideboard. There is a dark red plush tablecloth with an immense fringe all round it. She has some china shepherd and shepherdess figures on the mantelpiece and two stuffed birds under glass covers. There is a mirror over the mantel and a great many photographs in bone frames. One forbidding face glares from the cruet on the sideboard. I examine the room to try to overcome my uneasiness and the wishing to be with Dr Metcalf. When we were in the fog he was close to me guiding me with his arm round me and his body close to mine. I try to recapture the feeling of his arm being round me. Does he suddenly not want me? I wonder if he is in bed or whether he will come downstairs again. I open the door a bit but it is dark and quiet. Upstairs in one of the pretty bedrooms I would be near him. The time goes by very slowly. I am cold. I don't want to put out the light. Oh come down again please.

I feel I can't breathe when the light is out. I am too near the floor. Mrs P's horrible face seems to be in the room, disagreeable, when the light is off. I struggle up off the mattress and put on the light again. I check her black-out curtain and knock something over on the other side of the curtain. Perhaps a plant in a pot. I don't dare move the curtain to look. When I try to crawl back into the tunnel of bedclothes I knock over the water and it makes a wet patch on the carpet and soaks into the side of the mattress. The room is getting colder.

I am not asleep and, though I have kept on most of my clothes, I am cold. Right through my whole body I am cold. I wish I was at home and not here. I wish I had gone home. And another thing, I do not know where Mrs P's bathroom is. I want my mother. This is such an unusual wish that I weep a bit in a sort of despair. It is only a quarter to two. A great many hours till the morning. My mother would not like the Metcalfs. I wish I could be warm. Dr Metcalf obviously does not like me much.

The place where I lived as a child is a place of small mean houses in terraces in mean little streets. All around are pit mounds, some black with fresh slag from the mines and others covered with coarse tufty grass and the yellow weed called coltsfoot. There are small triangles of meadow with partly derelict barns and farm cottages. Sometimes there are a few cows and chickens. The bone and glue factory is not far away and at the end of the street where we once lived there are the brick kilns.

One night when I am walking home with my mother we hear someone crying in the darkness ahead of us. The lane is shut in by dark slag heaps and there is, as if relieving the endless smell of bone and glue, a sharp fresh fragrance from the elderberry bushes which are, at intervals, along the roadway.

'Who is it?' my mother calls in her soft voice. But no one answers. 'Who is it crying?' my mother calls again, her voice like a flute in the night. 'Who are you? Why are you crying? Don't be afraid. Tell me what is the matter.' My mother, holding my hand, stands still in the middle of the road. After a bit a girl comes out from the black patch of elderberry. She is still crying. She tells my mother she is Sylvia Bradley and her father has turned her out with only a shilling. We walk on together, slowly, while the girl tells my mother. The fragrance of the snapped-off and bruised elderberry is left behind and the smell of bone and glue seems stronger. With a heaving roar the blast furnace on the other side of the town opens and the sky is filled with the familiar red glow. We can hear the wheels at the mine shaft turning as one cage of men comes up and another cage goes down. 'Where will I go,' Sylvia Bradley cries, 'I've got nowhere to go.'

My mother never lets us play with the Bradley girls. There are nine of them and they do not wear any knickers. Emily Bradley, the next eldest, knows a shop where the woman makes rum and butter toffees. If you eat them they make you drunk, she tells us.

I must have been asleep, or nearly asleep. Sylvia Bradley. She was the one who cried so much that night. All along the road my mother tried to comfort her and to persuade her to go home again. 'When your baby is born,' she said to Sylvia Bradley, 'your mother and father are sure to love your baby. You will see, they will not turn you out. Go back home to them.'

I want my hairbrush. I struggle up from the mattress. It is colder than ever in the room. There is a draught along the floor. My back aches. I want the bathroom. I don't know at all where the bathroom is in Mrs P's part of the house. I go as quietly as I can, feeling my way along the passage to the door which leads into the wide front hall. The black-out curtain for the fan-light window over the front door has not been put up and a faint light comes through. Perhaps it is the fog making a mysterious misty light. It must be getting on for morning. I feel my way to the staircase and go up as quietly as I can. There is a landing where the staircase turns. The lavatory, which has an ornamental stained-glass door, opens off this landing. Magda explained once that it was there because it was added to the house.

When I come out, instead of going down, I go on upstairs and along the thickly carpeted passage. I can smell Magda's perfume. It is dark and all the doors are closed. There is no sound from behind the closed door which is Dr Metcalf's. I go to the top of the stairs again and make my way back to the sitting room. It is airless and colder than ever. I don't suppose Mrs P ever uses the room and I'm sure she never has a fire in it. I crawl back into the cold damp bedclothes. The fog must be seeping in through the walls. It is not even three o'clock. My hair needs brushing. I wish I had my hairbrush. I am used to brushing my hair before I go to bed. I have not been able to clean my teeth either. Trying to sleep in my clothes is awful. I'm tired and everything I will have to do tomorrow rushes in on me. I'll never manage. Because it is silly to wish for my hairbrush and for my mother I can't help crying a bit more.

I am afraid to go to sleep. I am frightened of being asleep when Mrs Privett comes in here in the morning. I don't want her to come into her sitting room and find me asleep.

Of all the girls at school, apart from Ferguson of course, Bulge is the one I seem to remember most. It is not that I am always thinking of those times, but when I do, I seem to remember Bulge.

The first and only nice thing I ever do towards Bulge is when I visit her after her appendix operation in the hospital at Oxford. I have to be taken there to have my ear examined and dressed and bandaged. Bulge is lying back on her pillows with her washing bowl beside her. She is supposed to have washed her face. It is not visiting time but I am allowed in because of being brought to the out-patients department. Bulge is the only schoolgirl in the women's ward. She has her doll and her doll's clothes on the locker by her bed. The other patients seem to like Bulge. Even the nurses seem to like her and they even have little jokes with her. They all call her Muriel. No one except me knows the name Bulge. She does not know it herself.

The ward is long and narrow and the beds are all stripped on to chairs and the patients are washing themselves in bowls like the one Bulge has. She looks different. Her face seems white and clean, like wax, and she seems to have lost her spots. She looks tired and, without her spectacles, she seems more childish. Her face, I have never noticed before, her face is round. Her hair has been brushed back off her face and this makes her look different. She even seems pretty.

'Have you finished with this?' I indicate the bowl and she says yes and will I put it with the others on that high metal trolley. When I lift the bowl the water splashes up everywhere. I have lifted it too high. I thought it would be a heavy bowl by the look of it but it is light, much lighter than I imagined. I put too much effort into lifting it a nurse says as she goes by. I feel confused and ashamed and the nurse says she had done the same thing years ago, not knowing the bowls were so light.

'I brought this for you to read,' I say to Bulge as I place *Treacle Wins Through* on the sheet. 'Here,' I say, 'I thought you would like to read this.'

'Oh! I say! Yes rather! What's it like?' Bulge raises herself a little bit. She looks in an eager but short-sighted way at the book.

'Haven't read it yet, not all of it.'

'Oh. You finish it first. After all, Mummy and Chris gave it to you. When they came to school that day, they brought it for you.'

'Yes, well, I know, but they're your parents. And you are in hospital. I'll finish it after you. They are your parents – it was jolly decent of them to give me a present. They are your parents, after all.'

'Only half. Chris is Mummy's Friend. Remember.'

'Yes I know. But you have it first. Go on.' I push the book with Treacle's boarding-school adventures, which I am longing to read, nearer to her.

I can tell Bulge is pleased. She fingers the book and smiles.

It's the first and only nice thing I have ever done ...

I'm shivering. I fold up my blankets and the sheets. I let myself out of the front door of the Metcalf's house. It is still dark but the fog has lifted. I set off to walk to the hospital. It is still not light as I climb the hill to the service entrance. The night porter will be somewhere near there. He has the key to the special door in the basement. There is a passage down there through to the part of the hospital where the nurses have their rooms.

The night porter believes my story about the fog. He says not to bother about signing the book. He says the fog is the best anti-aircraft there is.

'There's been no bombs,' he says. His wife is nervous in the night, in the air raids, but this time she'll have had a good sleep. I have never thought of the night porters, or any of the porters, having wives, and perhaps children, at home. Suddenly I feel ashamed because, before I found him, I was remembering that I had no hair clips, no hair nets and not one apron button. I was thinking that Lois, and even some of the others, Ferguson in particular, must have been helping themselves to my store of these. These shortages, as they are called, seem more important than the progress of the war. Even that phrase, the progress of the war, because people say it all the time, seems to have no meaning. As I follow close behind the night porter I feel ashamed of my own small selfish brain. His wife is probably alone every night scared stiff. And I cried for my hairbrush and then centred my thoughts on a hair clip.

We go down in the lift to the lower ground floor. As we walk past the glass doors of Lower Ground Radium I catch sight of staff nurse Ramsden. She is sitting in the ward office with a small shaded light beside her. She is bent over the desk, writing, probably some of the night report. She must have been moved there recently. I wish she would look up and see me and smile at me. I have to hurry to keep up with the porter.

'Ramsden,' I could say if I could speak to her just now. 'Ramsden, do you know *The Hunt*?' And Ramsden, her eyes suddenly bright with some memory of the music, would say. 'Ah! Yes. Mozart, the quartet. *The Hunt*. It's K458 in B flat major.'

As it is a quartet, and, if all four instruments leap in together on the opening notes, it would be too difficult for her to sing the first few bars. From what I managed to hear, when Dr Metcalf tried the record, I feel it would not be possible for the human voice, by itself, to produce the sounds. If I could speak to Ramsden just now I feel sure that is what she would explain. I would like to talk to Ramsden now about the way in which the musicians, in a quartet, play towards each other, leaning forward as if to emphasize something in the music and then, pausing, they lean back allowing the phrases of music to follow one another, to meet and join, to climb and cascade. I would like her to agree with me and to say that she knows about the serious expressions the musicians have while they play and that she has noticed too the way they have of drooping their wrists and showing the vulnerable white backs of their hands.

The porter, with his key in the lock, is waiting for me.

'You know Roberts,' Lois says at breakfast.

'Roberts? Roberts?' I say putting my plate of fried potatoes on the table. I am hungry.

'Yes Roberts. Roberts – Nurse Roberts.' Lois lights a cigarette. She never eats breakfast. I move her tea cup nearer to her elbow. 'Well listen!' Lois says. 'Roberts. She's been throwing up all over the place. Can't keep a thing down. Diet kitchen of all places. Can you imagine! It's the powdered egg. Just the sight of the packet is enough to make her throw up. She's fainted during Report too, twice.' Lois, after a deep breath, exhales a cloud of smoke. She nips out her cigarette, squeezing it quickly between her thumb and forefinger, as Sister Bean, clutching the registers to her flat white apron, marches across the dining room.

'Abbott Abrahams Ackerman Allwood ...' Nurses in various parts of the large room are answering to the rapid barking of their names. Some half rise from their places at table. 'Arrington and Attwood ...'

'Nurse Arrington!'

'Yes Sister.'

'Matron's office nine a.m.'

'Yes Sister.'

'Nurses Baker Barrington Beam Beamish Beckett ...'

'Anyway,' Lois says looking at me, 'long time no see, where were you last night?'

'Nurses Birch Bowman D. Bowman E. Broadhurst Brown Burchall ...'

GERTRUDE'S PLACE

When I see the visiting nurse cross the lighted verandah of the house opposite I recall without wanting to the navy-blue uniform of the district nurse as she dismounted from her bicycle. Pushing through the long grass and weeds she climbed slowly up to a small house in the middle of a field where scattered hens were industrious and apparently independent.

At that time I watched from higher up the hill, leaning heavily on my own bicycle, assuring myself that other people, for example, Madame Curie, had safely ridden bicycles right up to the time of confinement. As the nurse made her slow journey I thought of the illness in the house and how I could go down there and tell her that I could do all that had to be done. 'I can stay. Tell me what needs to be done. I will do all that needs doing.' Easily I could do this.

The nurse did not leave. After a short time I saw smoke rise from the chimney; she would need a fire to have some hot water. I remember that I wondered then whether the nurse would know to shut up the hens for the night. As I watched from high up on the hill I thought of foxes.

I remember now, unwillingly, all kinds of things. One small thing only, the sight of an unknown nurse going in to an unknown patient across the road, is needed to bring back memories mysteriously stored in such a way that all seem fresh and whole as if they belong now at the present time, perhaps yesterday, the day before yesterday or this morning ... one of these memories being the schoolgirl game of comparisons which I continued to play, silently watchful, observing my companions noticing the quality of their hair, their complexions, their finger nails, their uniforms especially the condition of the starched caps and collars and all the time secretly placing myself above or below a standard which I regarded as acceptable. When I stood then in the queue for letters I noticed the fat stomachs, the thick waists of some of the nurses and how their aprons were pulled tight across this bulging roundness. My own apron, at that time, was neat and flat and the memory of the sudden realization, one morning that this could not always be so is so intense now that I remember clearly the unfamiliar nausea which accompanied this thought.

Other things come back in quick succession, the wedding ring for sixpence, the way in which I heard what had happened to Dr Metcalf, the attempts I made to retrieve a letter I had written. On that day, in the bleakness, I saw little Nurse Roberts, alone and portly under her winter coat, standing at the bus stop with her suitcase on the pavement beside her. And then there followed the whispered reasons for her running away. Always a great deal of whispering.

The daylight, that evening when I watched the district nurse pushing her bicycle up the steep lane, faded quickly and quite soon the dusk became night. Across the field I saw the light in the window of the little living room and I wished then for the times when I was in that room beside the hearth. I thought with longing of the times I had spent there and how it was a long time since I had been there. I remained for some hours in the damp cold, undecided. I did not go down to the place that night and, because of what was happening to me, I never went back there again.

One evening as the lift goes up and I am waiting, it passes the floor where I am standing and I see through the little glass window staff nurse Ramsden in the lift. Really I see her polished shoes, I know they are hers. Her shoes are of better quality and she has narrow feet, narrow at the heel and the shoes fit perfectly as if made especially for her.

I never hear anyone call staff nurse Ramsden 'Penicillin Peggy' though she is very often the one in charge of the syringes and the needles, cleaning and sterilizing them, and giving the three-hourly injections. Everyone calls Ramsden Miss Ramsden, even some of the patients. Because she understands and speaks other languages, she is often asked in to translate for a prisoner or perhaps a Polish officer who can speak some sort of German. This morning during the surgeon's ward round I can see her laughing with a German P.O.W. He looks at her with admiration in his eyes and he carefully repeats some of the words and she, in her quiet way, laughs softly again and translates for Mr Bowen, the surgeon, and he laughs too. Ramsden is not at all nervous with Mr Bowen, she bends over to unfasten the bandage and to remove the dressing and the prisoner closes his eyes and grips the head rail of the bed till his knuckles shine white.

Ramsden reads Rilke in German. I have heard her read. Perhaps it is that which makes me invite her.

'Ramsden,' I say, 'my folks,' this is not my way but I say it, 'my folks would be very happy if you would visit, you know, if you would care to come and stay with us sometime.'

Ramsden says she would like that very much and she thanks me.

My mother would like someone who can read these poems in her language. I am always trying to think of ways to comfort my mother and it seems to me that I can offer Ramsden to her.

'Infection takes the line of least resistance, sing that to la,' Trent says, 'a peptic ulcer is an ulcer which occurs anywhere in the alimentary canal – repeat after me – a peptic ulcer is ...' This evening we are all trying to revise for our exams. Trent, with her uniform unbuttoned, is on circulation, Ferguson has turned up varicose conditions and Lois wants to go over the preparation of trolleys for mastoid dressings, lumbar puncture and washing a patient's hair in bed. Of course I cannot tell them that I shall be inviting staff nurse Ramsden home later on when we have some holidays. I can't help thinking about my invitation with a mixture of excitement and plain worry. For one thing where could staff nurse Ramsden sleep in my mother's house?

'Now gels, heads up, throw out your chests.' Trent opens the window. 'Mind the black-out,' someone says. It is impossible to study with Trent in the room. She makes a joke out of everything. She sings and dances and dresses up in bath towels. She pretends to give elaborate intimate treatment to imaginary patients. She pretends she has made dreadful mistakes and kneels before an imaginary ward sister ...

We have all started having cold baths every morning. Trent has one too but we have all noticed the steam coming under the partition ...

Lois says to me later that she has worked with Trent on the wards and that if she, Lois, were ill it would be Trent she would want to have to look after her. This is considered to be the highest praise one nurse can give another nurse.

Because of the war some wards are badly overcrowded to enable us to prepare others to be quite empty in readiness for the wounded. It is impossible to imagine a life which is not in the war.

'O'course we couldn't go to bed or anythin' – they had ladders great big long ones up the wall to our winders an' we hid under the bed, we didn't have any candle for fear they would see it and our shadders on the curtings an' all along the mantelpiece we had these big paint tins full of rusty old nails to rattle about and throw should any of 'em come right up and bosst in through the winder.'

I am at Gertrude's Place. Gertrude is telling me about what she calls the raids when she was a girl. She lived then, she tells me, in a Place called Netherton or near there just out of it somewhere where the chain shops were, and the women (her mother was one of them), with great big muscles for swinging a sledge hammer, made chains. Gertrude had to take her little baby brother to be fed, he was on the breast, she says; 'The women all set theirselves comfortable against the wall to feed the babbies and us girls we played skip rope an' hopscotch an' clay allys and such till it was time to take the babbies back home and put the taters on the hob to boil.' The women, she tells me, wore big overall dresses and they did not bother much about any knickers. Her mother, she says, did not know any life except the chain shop. There were different gangs she explains and they were always raiding. She says having to put black stuff over her window now at night because of the air raids even though she is in the country reminds her of when she was a girl and they didn't dare to show any light. 'I thought,' she says, 'that bein' here in the fields and with the spinney so close a light would not show but they, the wardens, they keep comin' to say they can see a light from my place. The wardens come here you see ... reminds me of them gangs years ago ...'

I am at Gertrude's place, it is the country. I came on my bicycle. My day off. I have two days off. 'I'll come again tomorrow,' I say. She is pleased. She is always waiting for me to come. She writes letters in big black handwriting on paper used for wrapping boiling fowls. In places her pen digs up the paper.

.. If you can come Tue or Wed ... I shall be home.
If too tired for the bicycle you can get the elevan a.m.
bus to the Holly Bush and walk down by the spinney
it's about a mile but it don't seem that long and you
can have a good rest ... I'll have some eggs ...

In the rush of work on the wards I am always thinking of Gertrude's Place and how I will get out there first thing on my day off.

I have been cutting out a frieze of wallpaper with rosebuds on it and we have pasted it round her back kitchen wall. Against the blue distemper the pink and white looks nice. Gertrude says she is pleased. I can see the way her eyes are shining that she is pleased. She is sunburned and seems old and she always looks clean even though she can only wash with a bit of rag wrung out in a basin of hot water. She does not have a bathroom. In one room there is a billiard table and the incubators and a harmonium which she plays while she sings hymns. She and her husband don't go to bed at night she explains on one of my visits. They sit one each side of the fire with the kettle singing. They sit there and sleep the night, she laughs when she tells me, and says that the kettle there on the hob is ready and boiling every morning. A big oil lamp on three chains hangs low over the table in the living room. The table is so littered with things never put away that they have become, as she says, so much rubbish. She clears a space on the corner of the table so that I can eat the egg she has boiled for me. She cuts the loaf on a folded piece of newspaper and hands me slices of white bread spread with real butter.

'It must be all your butter ration,' I say.

'There's plenty where that came from,' she says. And I describe the little string bags which all the nurses carry with them; 'a little jar for sugar, one for butter and one for jam or marmalade.' I tell her about the tin baths of jam made in the hospital and ladled into our jars. She can't imagine, she says, us all lining up once a week. I tell her about the black-out shutters for the tall windows in the wards and how these have to be put up early shutting out the sun and the fresh air. We have exams I tell her in about two weeks time. She says can I eat a second egg if she puts one on and I say yes if she can spare it. This makes her laugh.

I want to tell Gertrude about Lois, my friend, being jealous of my new friendship with Dr Metcalf and his wife. I want to tell her that I bought Lois a pretty nightdress so that she would not mind my going to Magda Metcalf's parties and how Lois never wore the nightdress but gave it to her ugly, stupid mother who is so greedy she would take everything. If I tell Gertrude that I buy cigarettes for Lois and that I minded dreadfully about the nightdress she might think that I am too fond of Lois or something. If I tell her about the games at the Metcalf's party she might think I am in what she calls bad company. Magda is very generous. She tells everybody that I saved her life and she is always giving me expensive things like the silver bracelets which I can't wear. For some reason bangles look all wrong on my arms and, in any case, people would wonder where I got them from. She has given me some pure silk blouses which don't really suit me. I don't know what to wear them with and then there's other things like chiffon scarves and lace-edged hankies and a jewelled comb. As well as all this she is giving me something else which I can't explain about to Gertrude. Magda tells me to come round whenever I'm free because they love having me there.

I can't exactly explain to Gertrude how they show me off to their friends in the strange way that they do. Magda calls me Darling in front of everyone and Dr Metcalf actually called me by my first name on the ward the other day. How can I tell Gertrude about these people; they are very nice and they want me to be with them. Of course I didn't save Magda's life. She was admitted to Casualty one night while I was relief nurse there. She was in an attack of asthma, it looked pretty fearful and because I didn't know what to do till the R.M.O. came I dragged in the big oxygen cylinder and Magda got better straight away at the sight of it.

'Since when,' the Night Superintendent said later, 'since when, Nurse, has oxygen been the remedy for asthma? And by what miracle, Nurse, can an empty cylinder be of use to anyone?' How can I tell anyone that? And Lois says do I realize that Dr Metcalf has made eleven nurses pregnant and don't I know what it was that caused Sister Green on chests to suicide.

I think I love Dr Metcalf. Certainly I love Magda, she is kind and full of ideas. All her friends love her and they dress up and cook wild meals and dance and, though I mostly watch, I love being at their house especially when Dr Metcalf lends me books or suggests that we listen to music. Sometimes he looks very tired and one night I thought he was looking at me as if he loved me and when he walked to the bus with me he caught my hand quickly as the bus came and quickly kissed my fingers ...

Gertrude brings my second egg and watches me eat it. Perhaps I will tell her next time and then give up all that she thinks is bad company. I think from what little she says that she does not much care for Lois. Lois smokes all the time and never has any money. Once when I mention the money side of things Gertrude says that she must have some because if the hospital is paying me twenty-eight shillings a month they must be paying her too.

'They wouldn't give to one and not to another,' Gertrude says. Which is, of course, perfectly true.

The sky always seems nearer at Gertrude's Place. It seems to come down, rain soft and swollen, the clouds rosy at the edges and shining as if pearls are sewn into their linings, to the top of the grassy slope which goes straight up from the windows of the living room. The feeling I have of being able to reach out to take the sky in both hands is one of the most restful things I have ever known. I sit there knowing about the nearness of the sky, not reaching out but, at the same time, pleased about the possibilities. These possibilities are connected in an undefined way with Dr Metcalf and how I feel towards him, and then there is Gertrude sitting across on the other side of the table. Two separate people but joined together because of how I feel about them.

The fowls are dotted white and brown all over the slope of the field. Gertrude has an old bucket on its side out there on the grass. She can tell at once when it starts to rain because of the splash marks the first drops make on it. A rooster struts by and Gertrude, with her little laugh, says to always watch that one. 'Keep a eye on him,' she says, 'don't trust him, not a inch, he'll be into you where you least expect it.' She laughs again.

'Roosters!' she says, 'they can be something wicked!' Afterwards we put the eggs ready for me to take home. Lovely smooth large eggs, their shells glowing a cream apricot colour or pure white with a translucence which makes them seem frail. We wrap the eggs in threes in torn-off pieces of a magazine. They are black-market eggs and my mother, anxious always about provisions, has said to me to buy as many as Gertrude can spare. She lets me have three dozen. She has two dressed fowls for my mother too, one of them she explains has had a fox get to her but not much taken, just a wing and a bit of breast. She has neatened the fowl, she says, with her dress-making scissors. 'Tell mother,' she says, 'I'm sorry about that old red fox.'

As we work I have a great wish to talk about Dr Metcalf, to tell Gertrude about his quiet gentleness and about his brown eyes. I want to tell her about Magda and how fond she is of her beautiful dog, how the dog lies in bed beside her, a Red Setter, and how Magda talks to him and fondles him. I could tell Gertrude I feel sorry for Dr Metcalf, that I want ... Gertrude says what about a game of billiards or cards. Games bore me but I play because I know Gertrude likes to play. We play racing patience, Gertrude calls it 'pounce', it is her favourite. We play three games and she wins them all.

The long summer evening is beginning to get dark and Gertrude comes down through the damp grass and nettles and cow parsley to the road with me. I walk with my bicycle. I tell her I will come back in the morning to scrape and clean out the hen houses as usual. I almost say, 'I'll have to leave early because I'm going to a party,' but I can't say the words.

'Two nights off,' she says, 'Eh? but that's nice!'

I turn round as I coast down the long hill just before the road bends round and I see her standing alone and waving. I wave and switch on the bicycle lamp grateful that my father insisted on lending it to me.

When I come home there is a telegram for me from the hospital telling me to return at once. The nurses' hours are being rearranged.

'I suppose it's wounded men,' I say to my mother, 'a convoy.' My face is burning pleasantly with the fresh air. She is upset and makes a parcel with a fruit cake and some hard-boiled eggs for me to take back.

'There's a train at nine-twenty,' my father says, and he says he will come to the station.

In the grey half light I walk up and down the platform with my father. He always comes to the train if he can. He tells me, 'You are doing God's work.' He tells me to remember:

'*Der Herr ist mein Hirte, mir wird nichts mangeln* ... Remember,' he says; '*The Lord is my Shepherd* ... *und ob ich schon wanderte im finstern Tal, fürchte ich kein Unglück; denn du bist bei mir, dein Stecken und Stab trösten mich* ... verse four,' he says and he holds my hand.

'Not in German,' I say in a low voice, glancing quickly to see if the other people waiting for the train have noticed. For my father it is not the language of the enemy but is the language for cherishing. I feel his hand holding mine and I want to cry and go back home with him. I am afraid.

'I don't want to go,' I tell him.

'It's God's work,' he says again.

The notice board in the deserted front hall of the Nurses' Home is covered with neatly written timetables. I am on duty at four a.m. I go up to the room which I share with Lois. I go in very quietly as she will be asleep. But her bed is empty. The black-out curtains are not drawn and the window is open. From this window, high up, I can lean, it seems, right into the black darkness which is the world. There is a sweetness, a faint fragrance of crushed grass as if it has come with me from Gertrude's place. It is probably from the park. When I try to breathe it in once more it is not there. There are no lights anywhere only the canal shines in the light of the rising moon. The moon and the moonlit water are inextinguishable. Two tiny points of yellow light far below are moving and stopping and moving on again slowly. It is a bus. A faint roar, as of breathing, comes to me across the black shadowed roof-tops. I close the window and fix the curtain.

Trying to sleep I think of the tranquillity of Gertrude's field scattered with hens.

'Darling, you are such a pet!' Magda said the other evening when I arrived late (after evening duty) at her birthday party. 'Isn't she just a pet,' she called out, turning me round and round in front of her roomful of guests. 'Isn't she sweet to come after work. You Darling!' she kissed me. 'And you still wear your school coat. I love it! I wish I had it.' She buried her face in the dark-green nap. I was not sure whether she was laughing or crying.

'You could have it,' I said, 'but I seem to need it!'

'She seems to need it,' Magda cried. 'Oh isn't she just perfect. A natural perfect! Jonty,' she called Dr Metcalf, 'take this dear child somewhere and undress her. Help her out of this coat.' They were all laughing.

If I tell Gertrude she will see how generous and kind Magda is. But Gertrude might think she is being generous with the wrong things. I do not want to give back the special thing I am being given. Gertrude I feel sure will tell me not to take.

I turn over. I am afraid because I can't sleep. Then the rumbling starts. I have heard this noise before. I know what it is. I watched one morning with Lois. From our high-up window we could see a long train of mysterious carriages and wagons winding across to the station nearest the hospital. This is what I can hear now. The wagons, some of them will be marked with a red cross, are bringing wounded soldiers. I can hear the brakes squealing as the train draws up and stops and then, jolting, pulls along a bit more to stop again to allow the stretchers to be unloaded into the waiting ambulances. Quite soon I hear the first of these ambulances, like on that other morning, come slowly up to the hospital. They come steadily one after the other. The empty beds we have prepared will fill again with men who have fear and pain in their eyes. They do not really sleep but lie with their teeth clenched and their hands clenched and their eyes half open. Some of them are not able to close their eyes in sleep.

I do not see Lois at all or Trent. We leave little notes for each other. We are working an eight-hour shift, eight hours on and eight hours off. There is no time off. We eat and sleep and work and eat and sleep and work. Some of the nurses get ill and we are short of staff. The ward where I am is all split beds for amputations. Every bed has its own electric bell and its own tourniquet, some beds have two.

Gertrude, waiting for me to come, writes to me. I queue for letters and am pleased when I see her black handwriting;

> Queenie has her pups you'll be pleased to know little balls of fat tumbling about you'll love 'em. If you miss the eleven am bus there's another at one. We would have a bit less time that's all –

and

> Have you ever seen the pig's meat salted down you'll see it up at Violet's when you come they've killed a pig up there you should taste the pork pies. I'll have one ready all wrapped for you ...

One of the men, he is only a boy really, as well as having both legs amputated above the knee, has a terrible wound in his stomach. I try, while I am dressing it, not to show that I can't bear it. One day he asks me to put the gold cross from round his neck into the wound but I tell him I can't do this. He begs me and I say no I can't because it isn't sterile. He has tears on his face and my own eyes fill with tears so that it is hard to see what I am doing. I brush something small and white out of his bed. It seems to roll up like a soft bread crumb. As I swab the wound it seems something is moving in it. It is a maggot. I pick it out quickly with the forceps trying not to show my shock. Suddenly I see there are maggots everywhere. It's as though he is being eaten alive. They are crawling from under his other bandages and in and out of his shirt and the sheets. I lean over him to try to stop him seeing and I ring the bell, the three rings for emergency. I have never done this before. I try to cover him but the maggots have spilled on the floor and he has seen them. I see the horror of it in his eyes.

The charge nurse comes round the screens straight away. 'Fetch a dustpan and brush nurse,' she says to me, 'and ring for the R.S.O.' As I go I hear her raised voice as she tries to restrain him and to say words of comfort – that the maggots have been put there on purpose, that they have cleaned his wounds and yes of course she'll put the gold cross wherever he wants it – yes, she'll put it there now –

Magda, who has a bad toothache, telephones me on the ward. Her face is horrible, all swollen, she says. She wants me to go with them to their little shack on the river. An easy journey she explains, a bus every hour on the hour. It is awkward taking the phone call in the ward office. I tell her I am not free. 'Well Darling,' she says, 'next week then, as soon as you can manage. We'll be there. Just shout from the bank and we'll bring the punt to get you.'

'Oh lovely!' I say, trying to get my voice as like Magda's as I can so that Ferguson, who has come into the office in a hurry for the thermometers, can hear, 'Oh lovely!'

All evening while I am cleaning locker tops and making beds and giving out the soup and bread the men have for their supper I think about the river shack, a holiday bungalow which is a part of a rich person's life. I can imagine it clearly, low on the bank close to the quiet water. It will be painted white and there will be a small landing, a wooden jetty, belonging just to that cottage. I have seen these places, very private with grass coming right up to the walls. And all night it will be possible to smell the river water and to hear the soft sounds of it. I can imagine too the pleasure of being on the private jetty, of sitting there with my feet in the water as rich people sit looking as if they own that particular part of the river while ordinary people can only go by during an hour's paid-for pleasure trip in a boat owned and hired out by someone else ...

Gertrude writes to say she is renting the field next to her place and it is for me. I can have some fowls of my own there and she'll look after them while I am at the hospital. She is buying some bricks too. She adds a p.s., 'p'raps we could build us a pig pen and have a pig between us, a sow, we'd make a lot from the litter. I've always wanted to keep a pig.'

I can't sleep and I try to read and I find a passage written by George Eliot to Caroline Bray after she has started her life with George Lewes. She writes:

> *I should like never to write about myself again; it is not healthy to dwell on one's own feelings and conduct, but only to try and live more faithfully and lovingly every fresh day ...*

I like this very much and I sit on the edge of my bed and write a letter to Gertrude. I tell her that I like the idea of the field and the pig sty very much. I want to write to her about the maggots, I keep seeing them in my mind, but I write about Magda, all about her, about her face swollen with the bad tooth and how she says she is such a cold person and when you go to see her she is all crouched over a fire with little heaps of underclothes arranged all round the hearth to warm. I write some pages about the excitement of being invited to a doctor's house and how Magda is the daughter of a leading surgeon and that this is a good thing for Dr Metcalf – everyone says so. I tell her about the all-night parties and how Magda and her friends call me 'darling'. And then I write about Dr Metcalf and tell her that I think I love him. I end the letter telling her that I'm coming over to her place on my next day off to clean out the hen houses and to see my field and I tell her that I want to see her more than

I want to see anyone else. I try to end my letter with a sentence from the quotation from George Eliot but do not know which part of it to include.

The next morning I address the letter and post it.

Tetanus typhoid diptheria and gas gangrene. Relatives, mothers and fathers travelling the length and breadth of England arrive at the hospital too late. They sit in corridors waiting for the first light of the morning and for the first trams ...

Our examinations are postponed indefinitely.

I have a day off at last and I sleep all night and, because no one wakes me, I sleep all day as well. Unable to have these hours again I feel as if I am wasting the whole of my life.

I wait in the queue for letters. There is one for me from Gertrude, it is the longest letter I have ever had from anyone. I read it quickly – wondering what she will say in answer to mine.

I am ever so grateful, she writes, for the fowl pen cleaning out but I feel very guilty as well. I am very concerned about your health, I will own up, I know you are a lot thinner than you should be it gives you a Ethereal Look and you should have the Perfect Health Look and not be overburdened with life. I should like you to have a few weeks out at grass ...

As I read it seems I can smell the potatoes boiling on the hob at Gertrude's Place and it is as if her voice is speaking telling me how a horse when he is overworked is put in a good meadow field, in good green pasture, where he can rest and eat and wander with other horses in safety and complete freedom. She writes:

I should like you to have a time of no worry and no burden.

115

I am thinking such a lot about you and want you here so I can get you better. I could clear out the other room and make a nice bed where you could sleep quiet and comfortable. Of course I know I can want this for you and you might not want ...

The slope of grass outside the window seems very close as I read on; it is as if she is speaking;

I will say that you occupy a place in my thoughts and in my Heart and life no one else will ever fill. Chiefly I am so grateful it will always seem so good of you, a person like yourself, to be friends with someone like me. I know I have to finish in this page and not be saying more in this letter it's nearly like saying Goodbye when I don't want you to go. I just want one more word. I don't know if you know it or not but there is something about you so refined and nice. Pure Gold or should it be Diamonds.

It is lovely to know one is loved and treasured and I want to say I am so Happy to think of you being so kind and willing to know me and to come and see me and write to me. I want nothing but love and happiness for you and complete Reliance in the spirit of one who loves you   from your loving friend

Gertrude

Though I am reading the letter in the hospital dining room it seems as if I am in the twilight in the living room at Gertrude's Place with her sitting across the table from me – the packs of old cards ready for our game. I seem to be in the silence of the late afternoon at her place. I am wishing to be there and I think how I will go on Sunday, my next day off. I will get up early and be there the whole day and examine the rented field and decide where the pig pen should be. Gertrude, in her answer to my letter, has not said anything about Magda or Dr Metcalf. It is as though they no longer exist.

'Long time no see.' Lois has plonked herself in the chair opposite mine. She has spilled her tea in her saucer. 'How's tricks?' she says lighting a cigarette and squinting at me through the smoke.

Every day I re-read Gertrude's letter. I carry it with me in the pocket of my uniform and while I am working I can feel its bulkiness. Perhaps when Ramsden comes to stay she will like to come out to Gertrude's Place, not on a bicycle of course, we can take the eleven a.m. bus to the Holly Bush and walk down by the spinney, it's about a mile across the fields. Ramsden will not be coming for a while. By the time she comes we might have the pig and if you have something like a pig it is nice to be able to show it to someone.

At last it is Saturday and I have the evening off before the Sunday which is my day off. When I leave the ward Dr Metcalf is waiting by the lift. He tells me that Magda has had to go off to visit her mother but the invitation to the cottage on the river still holds.

'What about tonight?' he asks. 'I'll meet you at the bus stop in about half an hour. A lazy day,' he says, 'on the water tomorrow. Magda will be coming later on,' he says.

'Yes,' I tell him. 'Yes, thank you, that will be lovely.'

Up in the room I share with Lois she is there, half dressed, smoking and flipping the pages of a magazine. I change and tie my hair in two bunches.

'How come,' Lois asks, 'how come the red ribbons?'

'My better-half,' I say, 'my better-half likes my hair this way.'

RAMSDEN

It is just like Ramsden, I mean, it is just the kind of thing Ramsden would say. She isn't saying it to me. She is saying that Bach must have written one of the Brandenburg Concertos in such a way that when a school orchestra drags through it it does not matter.

Which Brandenburg Concerto, I want to ask. But I am not in the conversation. Staff nurse Ramsden is talking to staff nurse Pusey-Hall. From the few paces behind them I can hear and listen to their words. It is clear that they have been to a concert together. A recital or a concert.

Bach dragged his violins as if on purpose. Only Ramsden could say something like this. So that, however badly the school orchestra played, it would not show. Ramsden and Pusey-Hall laugh in their well-bred way along the corridor. Like me, both of them are, in fresh white aprons, going on duty. Their long lacy caps seem to me to be exceptionally delicate, white and beautiful. We are all going to different places but this first part of the corridor we all share. Their voices are rich with amusement and tender at times as if intimate. I like the idea of the tender intimacy of their voices. I quicken my pace to keep up with theirs.

Ramsden is on the lower ground floor, a men's surgical ward down there, officers and men, men in the main ward and officers in the small wards. She kneels, at night, in the main ward to say the Lord's Prayer and the men, for those few minutes, hold up their housey-housey and wait in silence while Ramsden says the prayer and then they go on calling the numbers of the game. I have never actually seen Ramsden kneel down in the middle of the ward. I have only heard about it but can picture it well to myself. We are all meant to do this but not many staff nurses do. So far I have never been in charge at night but I try to memorize the Lord's Prayer, *Our Father which art in Heaven*, so that when the time comes I will be able to kneel and pray for the men.

Perhaps Ramsden and Pusey-Hall have been to something in the Town Hall. Perhaps the Sunday afternoon concert. Something quite beyond my reach. What did I do on Sunday? Of course, I remember, I went to sleep. More often than not it seems that I am sleeping away my whole life.

'An exploration of the twentieth-century religious belief and conviction ...' Snatches of their conversation reach me still. 'A need for the heroic response ...' I miss the next bit, 'the eternal suffering of ...' Whose suffering? Did Ramsden say Christ?

I am not at all on the same intellectual level. I think Ramsden and Pusey-Hall read widely, especially the work of philosophers, and they have been to a concert.

Miss Robson, at school, had damp dark patches under her arms when she was conducting. There was one boy, the leading violin, the only one of us who could really play. White-faced, I think his name was Mottram, something like that. It does not matter.

I think I know what Ramsden means about the Brandenburg Concerto. Everyone playing at their own pace, some ahead of others. It is nice to know what Ramsden means. I can imagine her at the concert. She will have seen the gleaming black piano keys thin and sleek on the white ones, and she will have seen the pianist's surprisingly short fingers. The hands dimpled and like frogs falling above and below each other along the keyboard. She will have seen his serious pouting mouth and her head will have moved slightly in time with his head movements. Perhaps it was a quartet or a trio, the players leaning towards and away from each other, the pianist breathing lightly with the sound of the cello. Then there will have been the repeats with changes from a major key to the minor and then back to the expected and hoped for major. The pianist will have flipped the pages, before the page-turner could lean forward to do it, to glance quickly at the bottom of an earlier page before bowing his head and playing softly, this time without needing to look at the music. And all the time the ardent violinist climbs with feathery notes and the cellist plucks his strings.

Miss Robson, at school, had a little rod, a bâton. She tapped it to start and to stop the orchestra. She used it to make us lift our wrists at the piano.

The pianist on the concert platform can let his wrists drop. His galloping fingers can be flat, splayed out, or arched. He can choose.

Ramsden and Pusey-Hall will know all this. Close behind the rustle of their uniforms my own uniform makes its little starched sounds. They have been to a concert, probably on Sunday afternoon.

RIVER SHACK

I have never wanted to spread out my pages to show to anyone, not even when I have been asked to. I have never told anyone about the little mark, the little cross, at the top left of every page. I never write a page of anything without first putting this little mark, without first asking a Blessing. How can I tell anyone this?

'I'll ask a Blessing,' my father always said before a meal. Because he was hungry he was always sitting down first. And, with his hand shading his eyes, he would bend his head down as if ashamed that he had started to eat before anyone else and before praying.

'Always ask a Blessing,' he said, 'before you do anything, before you undertake anything and then remember, always, to pray again and offer thanks.'

The little mark which is a tiny cross is on everything I write. I do not want to tell people about the little cross. People are suspicious. They suspect. They are superstitious too. They might be afraid of what they think of as the sentimental or the religious. This makes it harder to explain things. I have put the cross there for years. I never spoke of it, even in an imaginary conversation, with Ramsden. Perhaps one day it will be the right time to try to explain and, at the same time, to give up the secret of the harbour. The sky harbour, the exact place in the

Brahms where the soprano sings with sustained serenity, her voice rising above a particular group of trees on a certain road known only in this pattern of events to me.

If I think now about the fowls at Gertrude's Place and if the nurse did, in fact, shut them up early that afternoon when I watched from higher up the hill leaning on my bicycle, unable to make up my mind to go down to the place where Gertrude was lying ill – if I think now about them, it is clear that, shut up early and left, it would be some time before they were let out. They would be like the prisoners in *Fidelio* when they are brought out suddenly from the darkness into daylight, let out from the dungeon, at Leonora's request, half blind in the sunlight, groping for each other's shoulders as they try to walk round in a circle. It will be all that the hens can do if, like the prisoners, they have been confined in the dark for too long – just stumble about the field falling over each other …

If I think now of foxes it is to think more of their colouring than of their habits. Magda's hair is often the colour of fox, the golden red fox. A vixen. Gertrude would think of her as a vixen but not the vixen prowling for food for her partly weaned cubs or lying in a half circle of dust sunning herself and her offspring. Gertrude would see Magda as a huntress, perhaps hunting for herself, something stealthy and, though surrounded by people, alone.

When I hear about Dr Metcalf's death, a death without any sense I cannot believe it but I have to. The whole hospital is talking about it. He never even got to the front. That is what they are all saying …

I always lift lavatory seats and peer under them. It was Bulge, at school, who said to do this. It was when we were in the school sanatorium together, isolated with German measles. She said it was because there might be a snake under it. She said in Madagascar, when she was a little girl, her nurse there was very careful to make sure there was no snake under the seat. Bulge's real father was dead, she explained. He had been a missionary.

So now I lift the wooden seat in the lavatory behind the river shack. There is no snake. The door does not close properly so I keep my foot against it, but no one comes. It is possible to sit here and look out across the meadows. The early morning mist takes a long time to lift and disperse. And, in the evenings, long shadows lie along the grass.

I was not kind to Bulge when we had German measles. When she talked to me I did not answer and I lay down with the bedclothes pulled up to my head. She was sorry for me and thought my ear ache must be bad. It was embarrassing to be ill just with Bulge.

Matron seemed to like Bulge. Bulge did not seem to be getting better. She had pains in her stomach. The pains made her cry out aloud. She wanted me to call Matron ...

Magda's body is beautiful.

'You are beautiful,' I tell Magda. She is standing naked on the river bank and Dr Metcalf is pouring buckets of water over her. She seems taller without her clothes and I am surprised at her hips. I am surprised too about the size of her breasts. She is sunburned, a lovely golden brown, all over. The bodies of rich people are always suntanned and handsome. Dr Metcalf is brown too. It is because they can be in places where they can take off all their clothes. They do not have to look out of tall windows and see the sun and not be out in it because they have to work. The black-out shutters at the hospital are put up at five o'clock blocking out the daylight and the sun. People like me are always white. Even if there is a sunny day and I can lie in the sun I simply get hot and I stay white. My face is gaunt with the dark circles of night duty for ever round my eyes.

Ferguson and Trent go up on the hospital roof, the flat part, one day. They do not mean to sleep but just to have an hour of summer sun up there. They do sleep and both are still red. Ferguson's blisters are only now beginning to be less painful and Trent is peeling horribly.

'Nurse Ferguson and Nurse Trent,' Sister Bean said at breakfast. They both half rose from their chairs.

'Yes Sister?' as if in one voice.

'Matron's office nine a.m.,' Sister Bean said.

When I tell Magda she is beautiful she laughs and says, 'Isn't she sweet, Jonty, to tell me that? I'm old Veronica dear,' she says to me, 'can't you see how I *sag* everywhere. Look at all my saggings darling! Oh! *Quelle horreur!*'

When she describes her saggings she makes them sound desirable. Next to these magnificent people, when I make my comparisons, I seem to be badly made. These other people look at if they are the result of years of fine breeding. They are well-bred not only in their manners but in their bones and in their skin.

Dr Metcalf has his shorts on. He is bigger in his partial nakedness than in his white coat on the wards.

'Strip orf darling!' Magda yells at me. 'Let Jonty shower you.' We are washing ourselves with white windsor soap at the edge of the river. The smell of the soap out of doors has a curious effect and, if I close my eyes, it is as if I am in the night nurses' bathroom at the row of small basins, fashioning Sister Bean in white windsor ...

'Oh isn't she shy and sweet, closing her eyes!' Magda cries. 'Take everything off Darling!' Come on Jonty! Buckets for us both.'

The quiet water is disturbed momentarily by Dr Metcalf as he dives off the jetty and swims a few strokes round the slow curve of the river.

'Come on!' Magda says to me. 'You have this towel. I'm ravenous. I didn't have any breakfast before I left. Let's fry up the bacon I've brought.'

Magda's father and Marigold, an actress, come later in the day. Magda's father parks his car in the field opposite and blows the horn for Dr Metcalf to go for them with the boat. Magda's mother does not come. Magda was staying with her the previous night after having her tooth out.

Dr Metcalf and I have been in the river shack alone together all night. On the bus journey we were both so tired we hardly spoke to each other. He sat with his arm along the back of the seat. It was as if his arm was round me though I knew really it was not. I liked this very much. I keep thinking of the journey now during this quiet day on the water. 'A lazy day,' he said when he invited me, 'on the water.'

The day is anything but quiet. Magda arrives in the mist. Her taxi driver gives a shout from the towing path and Dr Metcalf rows across the secret water of the river to fetch her. I only wake up when the driver shouts. I feel all big and white-faced and puffy and ugly. I help them carry all the packages and parcels into the cottage. If only I could be a bit suntanned or else wake up pretty or dainty and not as I am in my slept-in clothes.

Some of the young men, Magda announces, are coming in a car later. She has masses of food she says. She has managed to get butter and cheese and real coffee and champagne and dried bananas. I am ashamed to be hungry. We sit on the jetty to eat our breakfast. I tell Magda I might be able to get her some eggs.

'There's a path up from the road but it's hidden in the long grass,' I start to tell Magda about Gertrude's Place.

'But Darling,' she cries, 'how divine! You must tell me how to get there.'

My evening with Dr Metcalf was over very quickly. During the walk from the bus stop, across the river meadows, to where the boat was moored under the bank Dr Metcalf was very courteous. He guided me from one firm patch of grass to the next. Enormous cream-coloured cows, their moist breath sweet with chewed grass, gathered near the path waiting to be herded for milking. He showed me the room in the river shack where I would sleep. Because the small house seemed to sit in a bed of grass, and because it was so quiet, I was reminded of Gertrude's Place. The house, like her place, seemed to be asleep.

'I never heard the river in the night,' I say. 'I had hoped,' I tell Magda, 'to hear the water slapping against the jetty boards, but I must have gone to sleep without hearing anything.' While we sit there, with our feet in the brown water, I think of the evening and of the way in which Dr Metcalf sat close to me on an old sofa covered with an unhemmed cloth. He said that he was older than I was and that I had all my life before me. He said he knew this but all the same he wanted to kiss me. Could he kiss me, he asked. I said I thought people kissed each other without asking. This seemed to please him and he kissed me very long and very sweet kisses. I think of these kisses all the time now and I wonder if Magda guesses and, if she does, whether she minds.

Dr Metcalf, after a bit, took me to the small bedroom which he said was mine. The bed was very low, he sat on the edge of the bed and held out his arms. I remember his kisses and I remember how he held me and covered me up. I must have gone to sleep without undressing properly.

'I never heard the river in the night,' I say, 'and I never saw the sunrise.' Once again I feel that, because of my work, I am wasting my whole life sleeping it all away, waking up all pale and ugly and not able to have those hours back. Dr Metcalf says it was a lovely sunrise and if I missed it, never mind, there will be plenty of other sun risings in my life. He smiles at me and my mouth longs for his.

Magda looks at me seriously and tells me that Jonty is right of course.

Magda's father and his actress arrive early. Even though not one of these people is in any way like Bulge and her mother I am suddenly remembering Bulge. Perhaps it is the outside lavatory, the earth closet with the wooden seat which I feel I must raise to make sure there is no snake.

When we were ill together, and isolated, Bulge showed me a picnic photograph of her mother and this person she called Chris.

'Is he your father?' I asked and Bulge explained that Chris was like a father but he was her mother's Friend. Her father died, she reminded me, while he was looking after sick people in an African village. Because of the boredom of being ill with only Bulge for company, and a few damp old books we found in the chimney cupboard, I stared for a long time at the picnic photograph. I tried, in the presence of *Clive of India, Bevis* and *Nineteenth Century English Gardens* to make a book out of the photograph. I peered at every detail, the tartan travelling rug on which Bulge's mother was sitting and the kind of cake she had in an open tin on her lap. She was handing cake to Chris. The idea of cake made me hungry.

'What sort of cake was it?' I asked Bulge.

'I can't remember,' she said. 'Perhaps Madeira,' she said. 'Chris likes that.' We were hungry all the time, both of us Bulge and me. In the photo Chris looked tall. He wore plus fours. He was crouching fondling a little white dog. Bulge explained it was a Sealyham. Her mother always had a dog and it was always that sort.

Perhaps it is this picnic lunch which reminds me. If I compare my mother with Bulge's mother it is clear that my mother is below Bulge's mother in the comparison. My mother has never had a pet of any kind. When I consider this I have to realize that she does not like dogs at all and would be disgusted if she knew of Magda's habit of having the Red Setter in bed with her.

Perhaps it is the tartan rug which reminds me so unexpectedly of Bulge's picnic photograph. Because of being above Bulge in my comparisons at school, her hair, her cracked spectacles, her complexion and the way in which she stood, bulging and biting her nails, everything being worse, I do not especially like thinking about her. This thinking puts us on the same level. I try not to think about her. Magda's father is very fond of his actress and touches her often. He is fond of Magda too and strokes her arms and gives her little hugs. For a long time he does not seem to notice me at all and then says he has heard that I am a Quaker and I say not a very good one I'm afraid and he laughs, throwing his head back, as he does in Theatre when someone makes a joke during a partial gastrectomy, saying that's the best answer he ever heard and then goes back to not noticing me. I can't help dwelling on my good answer and I wish I could say something else which would be a good answer. No one really addresses any other remarks to me and, as I am hungry, as I always am, I eat a lot of the ham and the butter and the dried bananas. Food rationing does not affect Magda and the food she has brought is quite unlike what we are able to have at home or in the hospital. Magda's father has brought a paper bag full of peaches. He has them sent from London. I have never eaten a peach and concentrate my thoughts on hoping there will be enough in the bag for us all to have one.

Magda's three expected guests, the young men who come to her house parties, do not come and she is disappointed but thinks they might come the next day.

Cows have trodden down the river bank but Magda thinks it would be heavenly to sleep out on the grass. Her father and Goldy can have the bedroom in the shack. Magda arranges everything.

'There'll be a huge moon,' she promises me, 'and Jonty will find us a clean patch of grass.' We carry out bedclothes out to the edge of the river.

I feel I should be happy listening to the river slapping gently underneath the weathered boards of the jetty. I am, at last, where I have wished to be. I breathe the river water and river mud smell and the fragrance of the crushed grass but it does not take away the unexpected sadness. For a time the moon is bright and the water, not shadowed by the banks and the trees, shines. From time to time something plops, with a small splash, into

130

the water. I suppose it is a water rat. I am wishing for Dr Metcalf, to be alone with him, in his arms, inside the blankets which are, like mine, rolled all round him. We are, all three, rolled-up bundles in a row, our feet down towards the water and our faces up to the moon. This is the same moon my father can see. In my loneliness now I try to think of my father and his moon but it is Dr Metcalf I want. I am thinking of him and wishing for his arms and his kisses. I want to feel him close to me again as he was last night. I wish I had not slept last night.

Sometimes a solitary boat drifts by. Though I can't see them I know there are two people in each boat, unwilling to stop being together and not wanting the night to end. The moon has a ring of light around it. Dark clouds hurry across the bright face of the moon. Magda and Dr Metcalf who were saying soft words, now and then to each other (they thought I was asleep), are quiet now. Perhaps I am the only person in all the miles of country not asleep. The cows, dark shapes on the other bank, move together. I can smell their grassy breath and hear when one of them lowers herself or gets up. I am glad they are not asleep.

There is a distant sound of aeroplanes. The engines throb as they come nearer. Like a heartbeat, on and on, coming nearer. They are German planes. I know this because of the throbbing sound of the engines. Far away across the water meadows pale search lights send their thin fingers, like long petals, across the sky. Magda says should we go inside and Dr Metcalf says no, what difference would it make.

Bulge, when we were in isolation together, said that the Germans, if they came with the aeroplanes, if it came to a war between us and the Germans, the Germans could wipe out Britain with one raid. At the time I thought that the Chris gentleman must have told her that. I believed it. Later we all said it at school. 'One raid and we'll all be wiped out. Really! The war, if it comes to that!' The Germans are not all that bad I wanted to say then. Not all Germans are bad. There did not seem, then, the words for this to be said.

Bulge's mother and Chris visited Bulge during our illness. They were so nice to me. Friendly and sitting on my bed and talking to me as if I had never been unkind to Bulge, ever. Bulge of course could have been as homesick as I was. Muriel, they called her Muriel, could have longed for her mother and this Chris. Her mother told me, 'Muriel has some rabbits at home too,' when I told her about our rabbits at home. Bulge was so nice to me. She never said one word about my not speaking to her. And she obviously had not said anything about the raggings she had from everyone. On the afternoon when her people came I hadn't got my spectacles on and, when her mother put her head round the door, I thought, for a moment, that my mother had come. I hid under the bedclothes when I realized my mistake. It was hard not to cry. It was then that this Chris gentleman sat on my bed asking me about my bandage while Bulge and her mother had their first hugs. I told him, 'It's a middle-ear abscess,' and he said he was sorry.

That night Bulge called out to me to fetch Matron because her pain was bad. 'I think it's my appendix,' she said, and was sick over her bedspread and the floor. I went down quickly, in the dark, to Matron's cottage. She came at once.

In my secret game of comparisons Bulge was placed high up, far higher than anyone else, for she had the school doctor at her bed in the night. I was envious and felt ashamed of being envious and tried to be helpful. Bulge was trying not to cry but her pain was too bad. Matron said to me to lie down and to try to go to sleep. She said they would have to take Bulge to hospital. They wrapped her in a blanket and took her in the doctor's car to Oxford to the hospital, thirty miles away. I imagined the car speeding through the dark twisting country roads to get Bulge to the hospital before it was too late. The tall grasses and the cow parsley along the lanes, I thought, would look like lace in the moonlight.

Matron, in her haste, left the light on and I tried to read the book Bulge's mother gave me, as a present, before she left. It was a school story about a girl called Treacle. The book was called *Treacle Wins Through*. I wanted to enjoy the book but I could not help thinking about Bulge crying and drawing up her legs because of her pain.

Magda's young men, the three expected guests, do not come on the next day either.

Dr Metcalf and I go for a short walk to the farm nearby for some fresh milk. We do not have to cross the river.

'I was hoping to take you upstream,' he says to me, 'in the boat. There are wild swans there, further up ...' I thank him and say in a small voice that it doesn't matter. On the way back he sets down the milk can and draws me to the shelter of a hedge. Quickly he holds me close and kisses me and then holds me away from himself.

'I can't give you all the love you ought to have,' he says and he kisses my fingers, very lightly, brushing them with his lips.

'That's all right Dr Metcalf,' I say, hearing my own voice and words with surprise. I tell him that it's all right, that I've got a boy friend in the forces. In the air force to be exact. We walk on back to the river shack.

All day I am wishing that I had gone home and gone to Gertrude's Place. There was no way in which I could let her know I was not coming. She is probably walking down through the long grass to look down the long hill, as far as the bend, to see if I am coming up, walking, leaning on my bicycle. Two whole days off wasted. I thought I could be happy just being near Dr Metcalf but it is not like that. I can't even look at him as I want to when other people are there. And he can't look at me, not into my eyes and my thoughts like the evening when we were down here alone. I want to be with him by myself. My mother, it consoles me to think this, might have gone on the bus to fetch the eggs and will have told Gertrude I am not coming.

Dr Metcalf does not eat lunch. He seems thoughtful. I am afraid he might be depressed and sad and I try not to show that I am. Magda is decidedly peeved. She says so herself. 'God I'm peeved!' she keeps saying it. The river is crowded with Sunday train-excursion visitors. Trippers, Magda calls them. She is obliged to put on clothes as so many boats are passing the little jetty. Young men, performing antics with punt poles, whistle and call out as they pass. Magda says she's had enough of the shack and we'll all go back to town and do I want to visit my parents because if so Daddy, as soon as he and Marigold are up and dressed, is going back to town and will give us all a lift and can drop me off at the bus station.

It is late when I get home after waiting hours for a bus and a train. As soon as I open the kitchen door my mother hands me a telegram. I have to return to the hospital at once.

'The telegram came yesterday,' she tells me.

'I would only have been able to stay for the evening,' I tell her. 'I've had my days off.'

My father says he will come to the station with me. We have to leave at once to be sure to get the train. He carries the small parcel my mother has made. It is a fruit cake she has packed and some hard-boiled eggs.

'The eggs are from Gertrude,' she tells me.

Lois has washed her hair. It amuses me to see the turban she has made with the towel. I tell her that her turban is delightful and that I have brought some cake.

'We're on at midnight,' she says, 'a special shift.' She does not explain further. 'You're daft!' she says suddenly, 'going with Them! She's as bad as he is. Can't you see? Those Metcalfs! No I don't want any cake.'

'But you don't know them. They're sweet, both of them and very kind.' I eat a piece of the cake.

'Oh yes!' Lois says, and then with an accent, 'Oh! yeah?'

'They're my friends,' I say.

'Some friends!' She lights a cigarette from the new packet I have brought for her. 'He's the reason for Smithers suiciding,' she says, 'it was because of Dr Metcalf.'

134

Smithers, the theatre orderly, I remember him reading a poem he'd written. He asked me if he could read it. And then he asked me what I thought about it. He was very tall and pale because of always being indoors and in the artifical light of the theatres.

Because of the charge nurse coming in just then I was not able to listen properly. Smithers went on putting drums of sterile gauze on to the shelves and I went on handing them to him. I had not been able to understand the poem and, because the charge nurse did not leave, Smithers was not able to repeat his question.

I remember the poem and I remember his suicide.

'But Smithers!' I say.

'Exactly,' Lois says.

SINGLE MALT

Suddenly I am reminded of my mother. Perhaps it is because today, in the distance, I saw a woman with her hair curled as my mother's used to be. This woman was standing with some other people further along the street. Because I knew it could not be her I did not go up there. However much a person resembles another person, and it is not that person, it is not of any use.

Perhaps I should, at some time, write down every single thing which I remember about my mother. Perhaps that is something I could do.

My mother, who always needed someone to tell things to, suddenly, after the death of my father, had no one. After three stormy weeks in a private nursing home she returned home to an empty house and had no one to tell her dreadful experiences to.

She had to live several years alone.

... as he is now made partaker of the death of thy Son, so he may be also of his resurrection ...

It is my evening off but I am not going out anywhere. A baby died today.

A baby died in my arms today.

The book I choose when staff nurse Ramsden says to me to choose any book I would like to have from her shelves is a foolish choice for me. I can never say this to anyone. My mother is fond of embroidery and would understand all the diagrams and the pictures in the book. She would understand the step-by-step instructions and descriptions; mount mellick, crewel work, Berlin embroidery, tapestry, gros point, petit point, ribbon work and needle painting, bead work, black work and all the stitches and techniques from the elegant oriental Tambour ... I like the idea of the needle painting. Of course I can't give the book to my mother. It is a present from Ramsden and it is my fault that I chose it instead of some other book. I mean she had Wordsworth there and Keats, Goethe, Rilke and ee Cummings and Dickens and others. That is the worst of being asked to choose.

It does not seem possible really, this evening, to go and see Magda. During the car ride after being at the river shack they all seemed to argue, in fun but not quite in fun. Dr Metcalf laughed about Magda's single-malt gentlemen not turning up. 'They knew all the single malt was gone,' he teased her.

'They never drink all the single malt,' Magda said. 'You,' she said to Dr Metcalf, 'you always have your tots and so does Daddy. Don't you Daddy?' I thought Magda might be going to cry but Dr Metcalf was stroking her arm and I saw all the little lines and frowns disappear from her forehead and round her eyes.

I watched the hedges slipping by, the cow parsley tall and lacy all along the lanes. I kept wishing the bus station was not so far away.

Magda was sitting between us. Dr Metcalf's arm was round the back of Magda and his hand, stroking her soft sun-burned arm, was very close to my arm. The back of his hand was against my arm. I told myself to bury myself then in the beauties of nature for ever. But then, like now, the phrase, the beauties of nature, had no meaning.

Magda's father, driving with a well-bred ease, had one arm round Marigold.

This evening I am putting my stamp collection in order, at least I am trying to. Some of them have come loose and have fallen out. I am unable to be interested enough to sort and arrange them properly. My head itches. I would like to brush my hair but Lois, who has gone home for her day off, has borrowed my hairbrush. I open my exercise books of pressed wildflowers, meadow sweet, saxifrage, coltsfoot, lady's slipper and star of Bethlehem. There is nothing I can do with them and, somehow, thinking about the grassy places where they grew makes me sad.

It does not seem possible to go and see Magda today, this evening. Not after the river shack. I wonder what they are doing tonight, Magda and all of them and Dr Metcalf.

I put my clothes drawer straight, fold and tidy everything very neatly, and make up my mind to always keep my white blouse and my good pair of stockings clean, in readiness, in case I get invited somewhere. That is the kind of person I am.

Magda has not left a message telling me to come, as she usually does. Perhaps something has happened over there, at their place, since the river shack. She did have a tooth out. Perhaps an infection?

My stockings, my good pair, are really quite nice. It must be really special to have a man roll your stockings with nimble fingers so that when he puts them on your feet they unroll delicately and smoothly all the way up your legs. Once, in a film, I saw a handsome man kneeling in front of a very pretty woman and, this man, he could do stockings like this. I don't know many men and those I do know, for example, my father and Dr Metcalf, I don't think they would ever do stockings. Though, perhaps Dr Metcalf might.

The baby, the smallest baby I have ever seen, is called Roger Keith. He died in my arms. This morning.

'Nurse!' the charge nurse calls to me as I pass the end of Obstetrics. Ward 4. I am only on that corridor because the lift isn't working. 'Have you got a clean apron on?' she bawls. I shout back that it isn't very clean and that I'm on my way to Pharmacy.

'Is there something you need from Pharmacy?' I go towards her. 'They forgot our carbolic.'

'Take it off,' the charge nurse says, 'your apron, take it off and put it on inside out. And be quick and come along in here. Put your ration jars down there, yes, just down there by the door. That's it, turn your apron, quick as you can. Look sharp!'

The charge nurse is not one that I know. I don't even know her name.

'I'm not on this ward,' I begin to tell her.

'I know. I know that,' she says. 'It's an emergency,' she tells me. 'I haven't a single nurse free, we're flat out, three heads showing and five just post-natal and now this. Only keep you a minute. Quick as you can nurse, there's a good girl, you've got your sleeves down and your cuffs. Good!'

Propped up in the bed in the screened-off corner of the ward is a woman. Her hair is brushed back and tied up neatly with a piece of cotton bandage. She is very pale and she is weeping. She is crying without any sound, her tears are overflowing as if straight from her heart. She is weeping as if she will never be able to stop. The charge nurse goes over to her at once.

'The chaplain is coming at once,' she says in a low voice. The woman nods and still her tears pour down her cheeks.

At the side of the bed is a hospital cot, a little wire basket, covered with some folded pieces of flannel. The charge nurse picks up the quiet baby.

'Caesarian,' she says to me out of the side of her mouth.

'Nurse here,' she turns to the woman in the bed, 'nurse will be Godmother.'

'But,' I say, 'but I'm not a ... I'm a ... we don't ...'

'Never mind, nurse, whatever you are or whatever you do or don't do. Here's the Reverend himself.' Swiftly she wraps the baby in a white cloth and gives him to me.

The tiny bundle is light in my arms. His eyes are closed and his little mouth is puckered. Already the finely made delicate lips are blue. As I hold him close I feel his tiny body make a feeble movement.

The chaplain bends his white head over his book. He moves closer as he reads. He asks me to name the baby. I glance at the woman. 'Roger Keith,' she hardly moves her lips.

'Roger Keith,' I say, holding the baby towards the drops of water which fall like cold tears from the chaplain's fingers.

Roger Keith.

'*I baptize thee in the Name of the Father, and of the Son, and of the Holy Ghost.*'

'Amen,' the charge nurse kneels, so I kneel with the baby. The chaplain's words rush on:

'*... And we humbly beseech thee to grant, that as he is now made partaker of the death of thy Son, so he may be also of his resurrection ...*'

The small rustling sigh which was Roger Keith's breathing has stopped. The charge nurse takes him from me and replaces him gently in his cot. The woman in the bed holds out her hands to me and I feel their hot dryness. Her tears, like shining beads, force their way still from under her closed eyelids.

'Thank you nurse,' the charge nurse has escorted the chaplain to the ward doors. 'Whyever,' she asks, 'whyever are you taking your butter and jam and sugar down to the Pharmacy?'

'It's my morning-tea break,' I say. 'I'm to go to Pharmacy on the way back.'

The lift is working now and I go down to the basement in the company of a long trolley rattling a dozen chipped enamelled cans. The cans all have lids and they are all marked with numbers to show which wards they belong to.

'Sweet pees,' the porter says to me. He lights a cigarette. Porters, with trolleys and dustbins and theatre bins and laundry and these smaller cans, often smoke. They say they are allowed to because of the nature of their work. He is taking the urine from patients, soldiers, who have been having penicillin, to the lab. The penicillin will be extracted and used again. He tells me this and I let him even though I already know it.

'It's a miracle,' the porter says.

'Yes, it is,' I say and I almost ask him what kind of God there could be who would receive a child over whom the right words had been said and whether this same God would reject, really refuse, one who lacked this charm.

'Ladies hats underwear and dresses,' the porter opens the lift to a row of bins. Pharmacy is just to the right and the Laboratory a bit further on. We go along the corridor unable to speak because of the rattling of the cans.

I suppose they will be having dinner now at Magda's, perhaps something which can be eaten on cushions on the floor.

'Hobbling along supported by acadeemia.' Magda, frowning and weary, once more, in the car during the drive from the river shack, accused Dr Metcalf, talking about someone, a friend of his, a one-time friend of his, someone I have never met. 'She's done enough,' Magda said, 'to make herself a footnote in the literary history of this country.'

Dr Metcalf laughed at this, at Magda's supposed anger. He raised his eyebrows in an amused look at me across the back of Magda's head. He pursed his lips at me as if to blow a little kiss in my direction.

'That's not true, is it?' His tone to me was playful.

'I'm afraid I don't know her,' I said and I turned to stare harder into the hedges. Wild roses I wanted to say to them.

Look you, dog roses, hundreds of little wild roses all along the hedges.

'Darling!' Magda said then. 'Of course you don't know. Jonty had a Friend, with a capital F, who used to come. She said she actually thought our house was a sort of religious retreat. Can you imagine! A past pillar of the Ballet Rambert she wasn't slow on the single malt either. She ended up, my deah, in the school of stitchery and lace, an adventitious ornament, no doubt, with her big hands and feet.'

They all laughed then. I couldn't ask what single malt meant. What it was. Something hard to get, I supposed, even for Magda for whom rationing did not seem to exist. Something hard to get so that it mattered if their friends were not slow on it.

Because I could not understand and because I did not understand the metaphor, if it was a metaphor, the school of stitchery and lace, I turned away to stare once more at the roadside and at the trees in the hedgerows.

'Darling Child!' Magda cried. 'Jonty!' she said, 'I do believe our Precious Child is jealous. Oh you sweet Darling!' She broke loose from Dr Metcalf's arm and drew me to her sweet-smelling soft breasts and kissed me hard on the mouth.

'You are so sweet,' she purred and continued to hug me and call me sweet for the rest of the journey. So it is strange, very strange, that I have not heard from her.

DIET KITCHEN

'He didn't go, he didn't really go to the Front at all he shot his knee caps off and bled to death at his mother's place.'

'Disgusting.'

'I didn't know he had a mother.'

'Yes, the poor thing – even though she's a prostitute.'

'She must be quite old, I mean, if she's his mother.'

'She is. But some men, they like Experience. Experience counts.'

'That's right. Doesn't matter what sort of old bag. I mean looks just aren't in it. A man who's never done it doesn't go for looks, all he wants is a friendly vagina.'

'I suppose he was illegitimate. Anyone got any butter left?'

'A bastard. Hm!'

'Yes a bass-tarrdd.'

'Anybody got a ciggy? Lois brings her coffee to the table. She is on night duty too. I slip the new packet from my pocket on to her lap. We always seem to be having our meal times at the same time. Without seeming to notice the *State Express* Lois does notice. She clears a corner of the table for herself and opens the packet.

'How clean you are like a spring flower, a snowdrop,' Lois said to me once. It was as if we were in another world then. We were walking in the rain and we stopped suddenly, looking at each other and laughing.

'Your hair!' she said then, 'it's soaked but you look so nice, clean, green and white, they're your colours, a snowdrop. I'd like to paint you. Lois painted, water colours, in the room we shared. We pinned up the paintings even after the Home Sister left a note telling us to take them down.

'Your tartan dress,' I said, 'it's so funny. I like your clothes, they make me laugh. Your hair,' I said, 'your hair's wet too. This rain!' The unexpected rain made the tartan wet so that it was smooth round her breasts. 'Very sweet you are. Did you know you are very sweet?' I said then.

'Well of course if it's Dr Metcalf you're talking about.' Lois sends a cloud of smoke across the shepherd's pie and the baked apples.

It is Dr Metcalf. Everyone's talking about him, everyone, that is, except me.

'They say he never got to the Front. He was crushed behind a lorry, an army lorry reversing. And the war practically over too.'

'They say he was at the camp near Swindon. Ever heard of Swindon? Whatever made him join up now. Never got to any action. I mean if there is any now. It's too late. I suppose that's why. Pass the salt please.'

'Did you know he was on morphia? Used to come to Lower Ground Radium for it and whatsaname, heroin. We used to hide the keys. On nights, you know, we hid the keys.'

'Remember Foss? Wasn't Foss on Lower Ground Radium?'

'Yes, Foss was on there then. Charge on nights. Used to hide the keys in her bra. Ugh! This apple's sour! He got them, the keys, one night. When she was doing the linen cupboard. Put his hand right down her bra. Disgusting!'

'He didn't need to go. Have some of my sugar, I don't use it all. He only joined up to get away from his wife.'

'And other people. Thanks, anyone else going to borrow some sugar? And other people. He's made eleven nurses pregnant.'

'Could be twelve.' Lois hardly looks up as she speaks.

'His wife's twenty years older than him. Or is it thirty?'

146

'He's got nine children all with different mothers.'

'No wonder he wanted to get right away.'

'And some there be who've got VD!'

'He did have VD, you know, and must've passed it on to goodness knows how many people.'

'Should have gone to the clinic.'

'He did under an assumed name but quite a few people recognized him of course.'

'His wife's riddled with it.'

'Not surprising.'

'He wasn't a qualified doctor at all they've found out. He was just one big fraud. He was a greengrocer really with this prostitute of a mother. She worked in the shop and took the men upstairs.'

'That's right! No papers.'

'They found papers on him but they must've been stolen. He had Chatwyn Brown's papers.'

'Chatters Brown? But he was reported missing ages ago! Poor old Chatters!'

'Yes. Well, Metcalf had *his* papers – on him!'

'They found a dead German's finger in his pocket, too, with a big gold ring on it. Couldn't get the ring off.'

'I thought he didn't get to the Front.'

'He didn't. Probably stole the finger from someone. Had to take the whole finger to get the ring.'

'Disgusting!'

'Yes, disgusting.'

'What d'you expect!'

'Sister Whatsaname on chests suicided because of him.'

'Yes, and that's why Roberts ran away. Remember little Nurse Roberts? Ever such a quiet little person. Probably dropped her bundle by now. Anyone know what she got?'

'Twins. Could be twins, you know.'

'Could be infected too.'

'Yes could be. Would be tertiary, don't you see.'

'Roberts hasn't gone yet. She's cutting it a bit fine. I mean it's

147

obvious isn't it. I mean she's *showing*.'

'And Smithers. Remember Smithers?' Lois looks for matches for her second cigarette. She glances at me through her cloud of smoke. Her eyes glitter beneath partly lowered lids. She looks away quickly.

'Smithers,' she says, 'on theatre, he suicided. Remember? Lemmington Frazier's rectal orderly. He suicided because of Metcalf.'

'Lemmington Frazier! That's Metcalf's father-in-law surely.'

'Yes, he's on his tenth actress. Marigold Bray.'

'You nursed her mother on Women's Surgical didn't you?' Lois inhales deeply, holds the smoke and lets it out across the table. 'Didn't you?' she says to me.

'Yes,' I say. 'I did, Mrs Bray, a hernia.'

I often think of Mrs Bray. I remember her telling me that she worked at the public baths. I remember all too clearly that I cried by her bed, behind the screens, the day Dr Metcalf told me he was leaving for the Front.

'I don't want to lose you,' I told him when he said he had to go. 'I'm frightened,' I said.

'Don't cry, please don't cry,' he said.

'Don't you cry, dear,' Mrs Bray said, 'he'll come back. Your boy'll come back.' Mrs Bray said something else too that day. She said a person has to love work. You have to love your work. She loved hers, she said, at the public baths.

I told her I had met Marigold at the river shack. 'You know,' I said to her, 'Dr Metcalf's place on the river.'

'Oh yes, Edna, my daughter,' she said, 'only she don't call herself Edna any more. I'm hoping,' she said, 'as she'll come back and see me one of these days. I just have the one girl. That's what I mean about work. See? Enjoying your work makes you enjoy your life. Helps you to forget things as go wrong.'

I am thinking now about Mrs Bray's thin, sad face and how her eyes brightened when she talked about Marigold. I would like to talk to someone about Dr Metcalf.

'Mrs Lemmington Frazier,' Lois stabs out her third cigarette.

'Sweet. She's really sweet. Nursed her hysterectomy.'

'Lemmington Frazier! Gives me the shivers. Dirty old man!'

'She had her veins done too. Mrs Lemmington Frazier.'

'Yes that's right, she did.'

'Mrs Lemmington Frazier used to come round the wards with that Red Cross trolley. Remember? Library books and magazines and writing paper.'

'Yes and home-made face flannels and jam.'

'She used to get chocolate and cigarettes for the men.'

'The officers you mean.'

'No, the men. She went round them all.'

'Her daughter, Mrs Metcalf, used to go too.'

'Never!'

'Yes she did, all tarted up to kill. You can just see it next to the Lemmington Frazier tweeds! A sort of heather mixture.'

'And the lilac twin set.'

'And the pearls.'

'And the lisle stockings.'

'But really Mrs Lemmington Frazier has very good taste!'

'Yes, if you like Henry Heath hats.'

'It's supposed to be good for a doctor's career if he can get married to a surgeon's daughter. Specially an only one. Promotion eh? Luxurious! Straight to the top!'

'That's right.'

'Wasn't Metcalf Lemmington Frazier's dresser?'

'Yes he was, that's right.'

'Lemmington Frazier's daughter! She used to call him Daddy and there she was in theatre, all gowned up, holding the artery forceps or a retractor. Supposed to be studying. I ask you! And nothing on under her gown. You could see *everything*.'

'Yes. She used to leave when Daddy did when the dresser was sewing up. Other students had to stay.'

'Must've waited somewhere for Metcalf, then.'

'He probably ran out after her.'

'But what about Smithers? Haven't seen him for a while, come to think of it.'

'Yes, Smithers.'

'Smithers? Smithers? Was he that tall one? The thin pale willowy one? Used to be the shave orderly?'

'You remember. Looked like he'd been in the sterilizer all his life. Steamed. That awful white skin!'

'Yes, of course, Smithers. Suicided because of Metcalf? But he was a *man*.'

'Exactly.' Lois says. 'That's exactly it. He was a man.'

The cigarette smoke is worse as some of the others are smoking now. I feel sick and am glad that the meal time is over.

'Lois,' I said once, 'Ferguson doesn't seem to like our being together so much. I think she feels left out. Could we?'

'Furgusun? Furgusun? Who is Furgusun?'

'You know Ferguson,' I said. 'I was sharing a room with her till we requested the swap. I think it hurt her that I wanted to share with you. It would have been easier for her if I'd asked to go back to having a single room. I was at school. We were at school together. You see? Could we include her ...?'

'Well, you're not at school now,' Lois said. Trent heaved herself off my bed then and walked, half dressed, round the room on flat feet.

'Quack Quack and Quack. Quackitty Quackitty Quack Quack.' We fell in a heap on Lois's bed.

'Your breasts,' I said to Lois later when Trent had gone, 'are indescribably soft.'

'I know,' Lois said, 'Matron says I must get something done about them.'

'Trent really can do ducks,' I said, 'she really can do ducks.'

'She really can,' Lois said.

'Ramsden,' I say making an effort to keep my voice level, 'my folks would be very happy if you would visit. Ramsden,' I say, 'when you have been to London, I mean, when you have had your holiday, I mean, I shall have my holidays then.'

I renew my invitation to Ramsden to come and stay for a few

days. Staff nurse Ramsden. We are in the lower ground corridor going in opposite directions. I have had my meal and she is going to hers. I have never worked with Ramsden. The others say she is very nice to work with. She is on Lower Ground Radium.

Ramsden says thank you and accepts. She seems shy. She often seems shy. It is then that she gives me the poems.

'I have no right to give you these,' she says, 'but here they are anyway.'

'Thank you,' I say, 'thank you very much.' I hold the little book carefully in both hands, with both hands together as if for a prayer.

'Look at them, if you care to, some time,' Ramsden says, her eyes darker because she is shy. 'When you have a minute. No!' she puts her hands over mine, 'there isn't time now. Put them in your pocket. Put them away.'

We both have to hurry.

'There is never time,' she says. She explains that she has had to leave the Junior in charge as her second-year nurse had to go off. 'She was really not well enough to be on duty.' Ramsden has a reputation for thoughtfulness.

Wherever in my mother's house can staff nurse Ramsden sleep?

The feathers of the willow
Are half of them grown yellow
Above the swelling stream;

I do look quickly into Ramsden's little book. It is all written in her neat small handwriting. Some of the poems are her own and some she has chosen.

The wireless is still on in the Lower Ground Men's Surgical. It is an officers' ward and the ordinary hospital rules do not apply. The lights are all on still and the officers are not even in their pyjamas yet. Some are playing cards and others are sitting in the ward office with the Charge Nurse and her Junior. All very casual. They seem to be mostly convalescents. The wireless is loud, 'In the Mood' is on. The lines of the poem seem to fit this music as it goes on and on;

And ragged are the bushes,
and rusty now the rushes,
and wild the clouded gleam.

The words in my head are in time to the music. I even seem to walk in time to it. This music 'In the Mood' is incredibly vulgar accepting, as it seems to do, entirely unacceptable vulgarity. I wish the poem did not fit and that I could walk to a different rhythm.

I wonder what other poems Ramsden has chosen. The Lower Ground corridor is dark beyond the ward. The poem is about the autumn. It's the beginning of the autumn.

This summer belongs to us you said. You told me not to call you Dr Metcalf. 'Jonathon,' you said. I was to call you Jonathon. It was hard for me to change. Dr Metcalf I called your name and you said, 'Jonathon, remember? Especially when we are loving each other. How can I be doctor?' you said. 'Jonathon,' I said.

For a few minutes just now in the corridor while I looked at Ramsden's poems I forgot, for just those few minutes what has happened to Dr Metcalf.

The diet kitchen is awful. I can't stand the diet kitchen. It is on the Lower Ground corridor further on from Radium Therapy and the Officers' Ward. It is a basement really and is vaulted. It is not well lit at night. I suppose to save electricity.

I am in the diet kitchen. All round me are the horrible little trays and their food labels. I hate cutting and weighing pieces of bread. I can't stand the smell of the vitamin B extract. The smell of tripe stewing is as bad as the smell of boiling beetroot.

I am in the diet kitchen all alone. This is the place where Nurse Roberts, on day duty, can't stand the sight of the dried egg powder, not even the packets of it. A kitchen boy comes in with fuel for the boiler and the stove. He comes twice during the night. He works in the main kitchens where there are quite a few people including a crippled cook who can't talk. Trent told me once that she has to work at night and that she hides during the day because people are afraid when they see her. At least there is company in the main kitchens but nurses do not work there.

The kitchen boy is waiting. He stands very close. I can see his ginger eyelashes, each one individually.

'Well?' I say sharply. 'What d'you want? You've stoked the boiler.'

'Is it God's honour truth,' he asks me, moving closer so that I can smell hard-boiled eggs on his breath. 'Is it true,' he grins, shaking his head and showing gap teeth, 'that Sister Whatsit up on chests and Dr Metcalf had to have a operation to get separated? Was they really stuck together like them,' he jerks his head in the direction of the main kitchen, 'like them in there says they was?'

'Of course not,' I say, 'don't be so silly! Here give me that!' I take the hod of coke and let it fall on his feet. His boots are thick and he does not seem to feel any pain. Either it's his boots or his stupidity. He stares at my tears. 'What's up? What's the marrer?' He peers up into my face.

'Oh, go away!'

'Orright, then I'm goin'. Orright. Orright I'm a goin'.'

'Don't cry nurse! There's nothing to cry about, now is there.'

It's one of those Matron's office nine a.m. things. I am here in front of Matron's desk. She is sitting on the other side moving her freshly sharpened pencil to and fro above a timetable which looks like a checked tablecloth in front of her. She talks softly to herself as her pencil pauses. She frowns, shakes her head and moves her pencil on, an inch or two, above the neatly ruled pattern.

Weekends have been the worst. Magda suddenly wants a garden Dr Metcalf tells me. She wants all the rough grass at the back of the house cut and then mown into smooth lawns. She

153

wants roses and fruit trees and vegetables. Weekends I have not been able to stop thinking about them doing the garden together. Magda wants home-grown salads Dr Metcalf explains. 'Come round,' he says in his most gentle voice. 'She wants you to come,' he says. He wants me near him.

'All right,' I say. I walk by their house several times but I don't go up to the door.

'The weekends,' Dr Metcalf says when we have a few minutes alone, 'the weekends are full of planting Magda. Don't cry,' he says, his voice very soft, his lips near my ear. 'Don't cry. Please, please don't cry.'

Matron says, 'The diet kitchen and, let me see, night duty I think.' She looks up from the big timetable which has, I know, because she has said so before, over four hundred nurses on it. 'Plenty of fresh air every day before you go to bed.' She smiles at me and tells me I am very pale. She likes her nurses, she says, to keep well.

I have never thought that I belonged to her. One of her four hundred nurses. My eyes fill with tears again.

'There is absolutely no need for these tears,' Matron says, 'come along nurse, dry your eyes. There is nothing to cry about. You know as well as I do that the rule about the doctor's corridor applies for the benefit of the nurses. Bomb damage aside, it is no place for my nurses. It has been brought to my notice that you have been seen there occasionally. No doubt you will have had your reasons and I am not going to question them. The corridor is absolutely out of bounds. The rule exists, nurse, because of those in our profession who are weaker.' She smiles again. 'I do not, for one moment, nurse, want to consider you to be one of them.' She has made up her mind, she says, that I am to be a gold medallist. 'You can do it! It's hard work but you can do it.'

I watch her pencil write my name in one of the squares.

'The diet kitchen,' she says, 'is not a place of punishment. It is valuable experience.' And working on my own, she tells me, is an excellent way of having a much-needed rest from patients

154

and other staff. She smiles again. 'We simply cannot have tearful nurses at the bedside you know.'

'Yes, I know. Thank you Matron.'

'I think that is all nurse. You will of course be, as part of your duties, dusting this office. I suggest you come in here either immediately before your meal time or immediately after it, between midnight and one.'

'Yes, I know, between twelve and one, thank you Matron.'

'You appreciate that this is considered a privilege. The dark polish is in this little drawer.'

'Yes, thank you, Matron.'

'You have weekends off. Also a privilege.'

'Thank you Matron.'

I must go round to Magda. I must go to the house and get my letter back.

An accident. The whole hospital is talking about an accident. About Dr Metcalf's unexpected death. The diet kitchen, because of its dark emptiness at night, is worse than any other place. I have to understand that I shall never see him again or hear his voice.

There was, this afternoon, a memorial service for him in the hospital chapel. I meant to go but did not wake up in time. Lois also did not wake up for it.

'I do have my principles,' she said. And how about we go to the pictures, Saturday. She's having the weekend off, for once, she said.

If Magda sees my letter she will be so terribly hurt. I must get it back. She must not see what I wrote.

I wrote everything to you Dr Metcalf, Jonathon. I wrote everything about us both that is why she must not see what I wrote. They will send your things to her in brown envelopes. Everything found in your pockets will be sent to her sealed in these special envelopes. I have seen rings and photographs and money and letters put into these special envelopes. The things are sent to mothers and wives, to the next of kin as they are called.

My letter to you will hurt Magda.

I love you I told you in my letter. I want you to come back now. That's what I wrote to you. I told you I was crying while I wrote the letter. Why have you gone away? I wrote that too. Come back please. Come back now this minute. I've been up to your room. I keep on going up there in case you've come back. Your name's still on the door. It's locked. Come back before someone else has your room.

I am sick, I told you. Every morning since you left I am sick. Remember I was sick? I told you I was being sick when you said you had to go and you said you would come back soon. And we would be together. You said you would find a way for us to be together. I wrote about that to you too in my letter. You told me. Remember? You told me to wait and to be happy knowing you would come back to me. Remember? You promised me. You said, 'Wait for me.'

Magda must not see my letter. I never thought anything could happen. I never thought you would not come back. Oh why did you go? I never thought that you would not get my letter.

In the middle of the afternoon I wake up. It is only three o'clock. All at once I remember. You see, while I was asleep I had forgotten. Outside it is bright sunshine. A bit cold. I remember you like it to be cold and sunny. I'll talk to you while I get dressed. You like it sunny and cold don't you. I'm going to get the letter now. In a minute. But first I'll go once along the doctors' corridor in case you have come back. Are you waiting in your room for me? Sometimes when I was on the ward, you know, making beds or taking round the trays at tea time, I'd

156

suddenly think you are waiting for me and I'd leave quickly. I'd take the lift and do you remember how sweet it was when you were there in your room? Sometimes I could only stay five minutes.

I'll always remember the time I stayed all night with you. You said there was plenty of room for us both on that narrow little bed. Please be in your room for me when I come now. Be waiting for me and smiling when you open your door. Please.

I have to go to Magda to get my letter back. You weren't in your room just now. I have to understand this. You aren't at the camp at Swindon, writing to me, either. There is a chance that you will come back wounded. You could be brought back, crushed with some bones broken, but not all that bad. Perhaps you are on the way back. Oh please be on the way back. Please.

What's the use? I must stop hoping.

Do you remember when you explained? It was such a sweet time for me, when you explained how you didn't sleep all night, that night of the fog, when you thought I should not sleep alone in the house with you, and you put the mattress down in Mrs P's sitting room. She was so sour that night. I hated her and her room! As if it mattered what Mrs P thought about us. But it was hurting Magda you were really afraid of and it was sweet when you said you wanted to protect me from your own feelings. Behaviour, you said. When we talk about Magda you explain so well that if Magda was a perfectly horrible person it would be easier. I understand because I love Magda too but it is you I want to be with for ever. You wanted me and you thought you should not. I feel very happy knowing how much you wanted me.

Magda needs you, you explained. I understand that too.

But the night at the river shack, I reminded you. You were lovely and smooth and sunburned and your kisses very sweet. You said we should have made love that night. I went to sleep, I told you. And you said yes perhaps that was a good thing. Sleep is a protection you said.

I am almost at your house. The bright afternoon makes me look

157

pale and hollow eyed. Ugly. I feel hungry but don't know what to eat. If you were with me we could go in to some place and have hot toast and tea. Perhaps they would let us have real butter and some jam.

It is awful to go towards that house and to know you will not be there. I wish you could be there to open the door instead of Mrs P. When Mrs P opens the door I hope she will let me in to the hall. Perhaps the brown envelope will be on the hall table. Perhaps I'll be able to take it quickly.

Why do you feel you have to go I asked you. The war is practically over. The war is everywhere, I know, but it is over. That's what people are saying. You are more use, you are really needed here in the hospital. The war doesn't need you now like the hospital does. Not like I do. I need you.

This is a terrible thing to say but how can I have proof that you are dead? Who can I ask?

I ring the bell and wait. On both sides of the front door the large clean windows are heavily curtained inside. The curtains are drawn. I ring the bell once more and wait.

Please, don't ever say that you can't forgive yourself. There is nothing to forgive. When I said that, 'There is nothing to forgive,' you looked relaxed and pleased. I loved you more than ever then. You said the hard little bed in your room on the doctors' corridor was now an idyllic place, that was the word you used, idyllic. You said that when two people loved as we have then it is as if that love is for ever. You told me to remember that.

No one is going to answer this door. It's no use standing out here. The afternoon is getting much colder. It's getting dark earlier now.

There is a queue at the greengrocer's shop. I join it to buy some Worcester Pearmains. One half of the shop is boarded up and an A.R.P. depot is in the boarded place. The boards are painted A.R.P. in red. The shop has looked like this for a long time. Today I seem to notice the boards and the red paint for the first time.

For a few minutes I forgot. It was biting the apple. Eating the apple I just thought about that.

It seems a long way back to the hospital. These mean little streets where we used to walk, hidden, because people we knew did not walk here, seem dirty and poor. I never noticed before though you once said they depressed you. You should see this street today. It is full of people, a long line of men and women, linked together arm in arm, dancing. Every day now there are street parties like this. They are like children in a school playground. Long rows of people dancing and singing. You know, the songs, 'The Lambeth Walk', 'Run Rabbit Run' and now it's 'Knees Up Mother Brown'. The women have got curlers in their hair and the men are in their shirtsleeves.

If you could see this dancing and rejoicing!

You said once how easily we accepted heaps of rubble. People, you said, got used to all kinds of things. It amazed you, you said, that this mess was all round people now and they did not seem to notice it. It's true what you said. There are heaps of broken bricks and slates everywhere and, at the end of this street, there is an old bomb crater which is not even fenced off. The people dancing don't seem to notice that some houses have whole fronts and sides missing. Some are tarpaulined and boarded up but others are showing pink and blue wallpaper, torn and discoloured. Sinister really, but no one notices. You could say a house looked like a doll's house, opened, without the magic. They have been like this for a long time. Part of the hospital is still covered with tarpaulin. Remember? The far end of the doctors' corridor does not lead anywhere. The stairs and lift shaft at that end have all gone.

This dancing in the street is how the war has been ending these days. Did you know, Dr Metcalf, Jonathon? Did I ever tell you how the war started for me? I mean really started. Not the declaration of the war. That was the terrible beginning. Terrible because my father could not and would not believe something which he had to believe. The war started one night with the post mistress and her son out in the village street outside my school.

159

They were banging tin cans together and blowing whistles. It was the first air-raid warning. We all had to get up and sit under the tables downstairs in the dining hall. And, because the post mistress had no other noise she could make, there was no All Clear and we stayed under the tables all night. You have never told me Dr Metcalf, Jonathon, where you were when the war started. Where were you? Were you married to Magda? I haven't had time to know enough.

They say it's an advantage for a doctor to marry the daughter of a well-known physician or surgeon. How did you meet Magda? I never asked you that either. There is a skinny black cat here. It's ugly because it's poor and alone. It's at the edge of these dancing people and it's trying to vomit.

Whatever shall I do with my life without you.

It is the weekend and I'm free. I have the weekends off now, remember?

I am at Gertrude's Place. Well not quite. The hens, I can see them plainly from here, are dotted all over the field.

'Gertrude is very ill,' my mother said last night.

'I know, you told me.'

'You haven't seen her for all these weeks, months. You've not been home to see us.'

'I know, I'm sorry.'

'You could go in the morning,' she says, 'first thing. You have to collect the eggs yourself and leave the money on the kitchen table. I'll give you change. Gertrude never has any.'

'Yes, I'll go in the morning, first thing.'

I am up the hill a bit from Gertrude's Place and I'm leaning on my bicycle. I wondered if I should ride it but it was all right.

The district nurse is pushing her bicycle up the field path. I ought to go down there. Perhaps I'll go back down in a minute. I have been up here at the edge of the spinny, for hours. Is it hours? It seems like a long time. It is all so quiet here. The nurse in her blue uniform looks small from this distance. I can watch

I can watch her disappear into the house.

I have been several times to Magda's, missing my sleep, to try to get my letter back. But no one is there. No one answers the door and the curtains are always drawn. I suppose Magda is with her mother and father. Perhaps she is at the river shack.

I keep thinking about my letter and all the things I wrote in it. There has been no message for me from Magda. She must know about the letter, and about me, about us.

Gertrude is all small and shrivelled yellow in a bed which was never used. She wanted me to have it once. I was early at her place. The fowls must have been out all night. I wondered about the fox. Fowls would have to be either out all the time or shut up all the time. It is something they can't do for themselves.

I watched Gertrude through the window. Her eyes were closed under a frown of pain. I watched and then I came up here.

I want to go back down there. I want to have Gertrude comfort me but how can I tell her everything when she is so ill. It should be me comforting her.

I think Gertrude is dying.

'I can wash Gertrude,' I could say this to the nurse. But I can't say to Gertrude what I want to say. How can I go back over the summer and leave everything unexplained?

In the evening I can't stop crying. I can't tell my mother. It is only a simple thing I have to tell her but I am not able to.

'You must not be so upset over poor Gertrude,' my mother says. 'She is very fond of you and she would not want you to be upset like this. Try not to cry.'

'It's not only that, not only poor Gertrude,' I say. 'It's because oh it's because I've been trying to write and I can't, it's just stupid, it's nothing.'

My mother is knitting very fast. She started knitting at the beginning of the war and now she is always knitting. 'No one,' she says, 'can write anything till they've had experience. Later on perhaps. You will write later on.'

'Yes, of course,' I say.

'You never play the piano now,' my mother says. 'Why don't

you go now and practise something and leave the front-room door open. I like to listen.'

'I haven't been able to sleep either,' I say instead of saying the words I mean to say.

'You must have some of my tablets,' my mother says, 'they are yeast tablets and are very good.'

'Thanks,' I say and I put my hands up to my face because of more tears.

'You promised to play Halma,' my sister says.

'Oh, shut up!' Immediately I regret my reply. I know she is trying to comfort me.

During the night there is a full moon, it makes a trellis of shadow and light on the opposite wall. It seems as if, instead of a corridor up here, there is another room. A room I have never seen before. L-shaped with a long passage leading to a place which shines as a river shines when moonlight lies across undisturbed water.

The tarpaulins have been taken off the bomb-damaged part of the hospital. This wing, at the end of the doctors' corridor, has to be rebuilt. There is no strange room there. Beyond some wooden barriers the hospital up here is wide open to the night. The corridor ends abruptly in space. The moonlight is on the wall of the huge clock tower which is a water tower. It is a reservoir for the water from an artesian well under the hospital. I feel afraid of the power and the force of the water in the tower. I can imagine, all too easily, the depths of the precipice in front of me. It is as though a neglected wound, which I already know about, has been uncovered.

All the doctors' rooms are locked and uninhabited. There are warning notices and barriers all along the passage. I have come up here one last time. The building work has started. Somewhere there'll be a watchman. Someone to keep people away at night.

The moon is wonderfully close to this ragged broken end of the corridor. I could step easily across this gulf straight on to the clean white moon.

The moon belongs to my father. He has always said it was his. If I was over there he would know without my telling him. It is only such a small thing I have to tell. Perhaps it is the small things which are the hardest to tell. They are the things which make all the difference.

It is because it will be so unexpected for him. What I need to tell him will be unexpected.

My father, when he comes to the station with me after my weekend at home, talks softly to me as we wait to cross the road. He admires the Clydesdale horses as a brewer's dray rumbles over the cobbles. He doesn't seem to notice the dried horse dung and straw blowing in our faces. The horses are fine he says and have I noticed how well cared for they are?

'How they shine!' he says, he can imagine the daily curry combing and the polishing of the brasses. The dray is loaded but the horses, moving all together, are very powerful. 'Look at their muscles,' he says, 'their muscles ripple under their skin.'

As we walk to and fro on the platform, he says even if we are not seeing each other very often he is always thinking of me. They would, he says, like me to come home more often. He is going out to Gertrude's Place tomorrow, he says, he is going to do a few things for her.

'That's good,' I say, 'thank you.'

'Is there anything in particular?' he asks.

'What d'you mean?'

'Are you worrying about something in particular?' His face is white in the autumn dusk.

'Oh no!' I say. 'Not really. It's just that I don't like the diet kitchen.'

'Quite a lot of life,' he says, 'is doing what we don't like very much.'

'Yes, I know,' I say. 'I know.'

There is a small sound behind me. I turn quickly. Perhaps it is the night watchman. There is someone in the corridor. A dark shape is coming towards me, a shadow in the red light of the little lamps.

'It's only me,' Trent says. 'I saw you pass the end of the ward.' She's got night nurses' paralysis she tells me. She has long woollen operation stockings on over her shoes and an army blanket round her shoulders. She tells me it's freezing on Women's Medical. 'It's that quiet,' she says. 'Kidneys. They're all on parsley tea,' she gives a fat giggle. 'They're your mob,' she says, 'you been fixing them lettuce again?' She takes my arm drawing me back from the edge.

'You lead,' she says. 'By the way,' she croons, 'has anyone ever told you, you're not cut out to be a corpse? No sex appeal!'

We waltz slowly back along the brick-dusty corridor.

'Do you come here often?' Trent, purring close to my ear, trips over the end of the army blanket.

'Goin' down!' Trent says in the lift. 'A-wun-a-tew-a-tree-a-fower-a faive-Tung Tung Tung Tung Tung Tung.' She can make a noise, with her tongue and voice, sounding like the plucking of a double-bass string. While clapping in a slow beat she taps her foot in a rapid rhythm. 'A-wun-a-tew-a tree a wun a woman band! Listen,' she says. 'Counter irritant,' she says, 'if things are bad make some other thing worse. Ching chang Chinaman givee good advice, don't pee until you have to. Busting! And that'll be all you can think about. Get me? And, just this, there's more than one pebble on the beach.'

I shall go to Magda's once more. One last time and then not any more.

I can't stop thinking about you. I think about you all the time.

Today I found out just what sort of person Magda really is. I said, didn't I, that I would go once more to see if I could get my letter back, the one I wrote to you. I was so sure, you see, that it would be returned with your things, the things they call personal things. I have seen Magda now. It's like this.

'Mrs Lemmington Frazier Metcalf does not wish to see anyone. She is not at home,' Mrs P says through the tiny space. She opens the door grudgingly so that I feel she is going to close it before I can say anything.

'It's only me,' I say quickly, putting one hand on the door to prevent it from being slammed.

'You nor no one,' Mrs P says. 'She's not in!'

'Oh please, please let me come in.' I am surprised at my own voice.

'Who is it Mrs P? Who's there?' I can hear Magda's voice from somewhere quite close. Perhaps from the stairs. She has a way of hanging over the bannister. Remember?

'It's me,' I shout. 'Can I come in?'

'Of course. Precious child, of course you must come in!' Magda is dressed in that dressing gown made of bath-towel stuff. She wears this only when she is quite by herself or when she is ill, she once explained to me. You will know the dressing gown, she said it was yours once. Her hair, unbrushed, is loose, all tangled and messy. Her face seems swollen and when I look at her my own eyes fill with tears.

'Why haven't you come before?' she asks.

'But I have. Several times,' I say.

'Mrs P Darling! Will you be awfully sweet and bring us up some tea?' Magda puts an arm round me and guides me, hugging me, to the stairs. We go up together. Her action reminds me of you, Dr Metcalf, holding me the night of the fog. Remember? I can't help thinking that she must have my letter hidden somewhere.

'Of course,' Magda says, 'I've been at Mummy's and Mrs P's been away too.'

There were no letters on the hall table, only the polished tray and other ornaments, all polished and cared for. No little heap of brown envelopes as I imagined there would be. She must have put the letter somewhere.

'I feel such a frightful mess,' Magda says. 'As you can see I've just let myself go. Awful!' She sinks down on the sofa and pats the cushions.

'Sit down,' she says. Her eyes are full of tears.

'It's so awful, you see, he went orf with such a cheap and horrid person. That's what I can't bear and Mummy, of course, can't bear it either. It's hardest for her. Mummy's really quite ill over it.'

So Magda does know, and her mother knows, and they think I'm cheap.

'I feel more awful than I know how to say, I ...' The words are too difficult. Magda interrupts me with another hug.

'You see,' she says, 'this person is really awful, cheap and I mean really cheap and vulgar. And, you see Daddy's so clever, a brilliant surgeon, everyone says so but he's stupid too. He's made a lot of money. Mummy's used to being comfortable. Mummy and I try to protect him. What I'm trying to say is that this cheap little person is a gold digger. Like all the others,' she searches for her handkerchief. 'But you, not having the experience of people like that, won't know what I mean. He is already, in a sense, at the mercy of perfectly dreadful people who are waiting to get everything from him.'

'You mean,' I try to say something.

'You see,' Magda says, 'he keeps making an awful fool of himself. Didn't you think she was perfectly dreadful? The last one? You saw her that day on the river. Gloria or whatever her name was.'

'You mean Marigold?'

'Yes, that's the one. It devastates Mummy every time – that's why I go over and stay the night with her every so often. She's dreadfully lonely.'

'Oh I see,' I am taking care not to look up.

'So incredibly vulgar and so grasping,' Magda says wiping

her eyes with both hands like a child. 'They, those sorts of women and their relations would take everything, absolutely everything. The relations in particular hound Daddy. And where would Mummy be? She dreads a court case and she's terrified of the workhouse. Daddy's compromised himself more than once d'you see – and now this Marigold! It's all so ghastly!'

We are both quiet while Mrs P sets the tray with the teapot and cups on a little table in front of us.

'Oh Mrs P, toast! You are a dear!' Magda can manage an entirely different voice. She pours out. 'You needn't wait Mrs P thank you.'

'Marigold's mother,' I say in a timid voice, 'is quite nice. I am sure she wouldn't, I don't think she is like that. I nursed her. Marigold's real name is Edna, her mother is Mrs Bray. She is a nice person, very good and kind. Couldn't you go and see her?'

'Oh mothers can't stop their daughters!' Magda laughs. 'You are so innocent and good,' she says, 'don't ever change!'

We drink our tea and share out the toast.

'Oh, I nearly forgot,' Magda says, 'you are perfectly sweet to write to Jonty. Poor darling Jonty!' Her eyes fill with tears. 'It's awful I can't stop this weeping,' she says. 'I see you can't either. They've returned all letters. I guessed you would've written. I've got your letter here,' she leans back and stretches her arm across to her little writing desk. 'In here,' she says, pulling open the little drawer. 'Here it is, this is yours.' She hands me my letter.

'You never put your name and address on the back,' she says, 'but I recognized your handwriting. Everything has been sent back to me.'

I turn the letter over in my hands, almost stroking it, feeling the firmly closed-down envelope.

'Thank you,' I say in a small voice, 'yes I did write.' My hands caress the thick secret letter.

'He would have loved having a letter from you,' Magda says, 'poor Darling Jonty. But as you see it never reached him. That perfectly dreadful place! It must have been awful for him and then no one being quite sure. It's all so stupid. Conflicting. A head-on crash?' She shivered. 'Dead or believed missing. I can't bear it. Really I can't. I've been waiting at Mummy's and now here.'

'Don't cry,' I say, 'please, Magda, don't cry!' The envelope is wonderfully smooth and unopened. Magda has given me back my letter. She has not torn it open to read it. She has not looked at it.

'There's some confusion. Where and which camp,' Magda says, 'everything's so confused. It's victory, I suppose.' And she sobs aloud and feels around for her handkerchief. 'In the front of that shelf,' she says, 'there should be some clean ones. Thanks Darling!' Magda puts her hand on my arm. 'You see, Darling,' she says, 'I keep hoping he will come back. That it's all a mistake. I haven't given up hope. I suppose you realize that I'm heaps older than Jonty. That sort of thing makes people talk, d'you see, they say cruel things especially about women who are older. Jonathon -' she starts to cry again, 'Jonathon, you see, I need him so much.' I watch her shoulders shaking and I can see the dark-grey dirty-looking parting in her bronzed hair. I know I ought to help her.

'Shall I find your hairbrush?' I ought to look for her brush. 'Shall I help you wash and do your hair? Let me brush your hair, Magda,' I ought to comfort her. 'Let me help you,' all this I should say. Magda would comfort me, if she knew.

She sits crouched on the sofa with her face hidden in her hands. 'You see, Darling,' she says, 'he wanted to be with Mr Smithers. Smithers went about twelve months ago to a field hospital and Jonty felt he should go. But you see, Darling, it's not so simple. People, men and women, will travel the length and breadth of a country, at times, to be together. In one way it's as simple as that.'

'But I thought, Smithers ...'

'They worked together,' Magda seems to have a note of defiance in her voice. 'I'm waiting,' she says. 'One thing I'm certain of. When he comes back, *if* he comes back, I'm never going to let him go ever again. I simply can't live without him.

Her long tangled hair falls over her endlessly shaking shoulders. In a blind dazed sort of way I get up and stand for a moment in front of her. I can't see her face, only her shoulders without an arm round them. The bunched chintzy curtains and the cushion covers, with their crowded little flowers and acorns, and the hovering perfume all seem too much. I move silently towards the curtained door and open it and, with light little steps, make for the stairs and the front door.

'How much are the rings please?'

'Them's sixpence. All of them. There's nothing over sixpence.'

'Oh yes, of course, it's Woolworths. I'd like a ring please. It's, er, it's for drama, a drama, for a play in a dramatic society. I'm in a play, er, Shakespeare.'

'Choose your pick. Them's all the same price, like I said, sixpence.'

'I think I'll have this one. It's quite pretty isn't it?'

'If you say so.'

All the lights are on in Woolworths and I move with the throng of people. It is slow, this getting to the doors, and more crowded because, near the doors, there are counters with a few sweets and people are still coming in as the store is emptying for closing time. Out in the street there is an eeriness in the sad twilight. The hospital, with lights showing, seems like a huge ship for ever in harbour.

Nurse Roberts, little Nurse Roberts, stout in her winter coat, was down by the bus stop alone. I saw her there in the morning. Her big case on the pavement beside her. She was waiting for the early bus, the one we call the workmen's. It was raining, a light rain. When I saw her there I never thought then that she might have nowhere to go. I was high up closing the window because of the rain. Now I think, where could she go? Where can anyone go?

The wireless is on in the night nurses' dining room. This inescapable 'In The Mood' music. It keeps on and on. Without wanting to I walk in time to this barrel-organ rhythm. Without wanting to I'm humming, without tune to this music. My voice in my head is an ugly croaking.

Lois is late. She comes in and sits down opposite me with her cup of tea.

Potatoes onions carrots, my ring flashes as my pencil pretends to scribble a shopping list.

'Night Fanny here yet?' Lois glances round quickly and lights a cigarette. She inhales deeply.

Someone turns off the wireless. Sister Bean, with the registers held to her heart, marches across between the tables. Her voice barks into the silence.

'Abbott Abrahams Ackerman Allwood ...'

Lois, in her cloud of smoke, extinguishes her cigarette. 'Whoever,' she says, leaning low across the table, 'whoever would ever have married you?'

'Arrington and Attwood. Nurses Baker Barrington Beam Beamish Beckett Birch Bowman D Bowman E Broadhurst Brown Burchall ...'

'Nurse Burchall?'

'Yes Sister?'

'Nurse Burchall, Matron's office nine a.m.'

'Yes Sister.'

'Nurses Cann Carruthers Cornwall Cupwell ...'

The Easter moon is racing up the sky. The stunted ornamental bushes look as if torn white tablecloths have been thrown over them and the buildings are like cakes which, having taken three days to ice, are now finished.

Tomorrow is Good Friday.

Next week I shall take the earlier train again and, before the journey is over, I shall speak to the woman.

It is more than likely that Ramsden would have white hair. Her hair was the sort of hair which goes white all over, all at once. Keats says, *to know the change and feel it*, I thought of sudden white hair when I read that.

The cardboard cover of the little book of poems which Ramsden gave me once, during the night on the Lower Ground corridor, is decorated with edelweiss and gentian, a circle of neat pen-and-ink flowers. Inside she has written in her neat small handwriting,

The best is not too good for you
Und Ihrer Weise Wohlzutun.

Ramsden, I shall say, *is it you? Much water has gone under the bridge* – this is not my way – but I shall say it carelessly like this – *much water has gone under the bridge and I never answered your letters but is it you, Ramsden, after all these years is it?*

PENGUIN – THE BEST AUSTRALIAN READING

BOOKS BY ELIZABETH JOLLEY IN PENGUIN

Mr Scobie's Riddle

Mr Scobie's arrival at the nursing home of St Christopher and St Jude – and into the clutches of Matron Hyacinth Price – is accidental. Self-educated and still preserving the gift of idyllic memory and wish, Mr Scobie stands apart from the others. For long-term resident and eccentric, Miss Hailey, he represents a kindred spirit; for Matron Price – a lady of questionable practices – the latest victim . . .

But unwittingly Mr Scobie has some recourse – his very simple riddle. Its answer – an ancient commonplace – jolts Matron Price.

Yet it is Mr Scobie's nephew, Hartley, and the group of nocturnal poker players, who ultimately change Matron Price's establishment . . .

Woman in a Lampshade

In this masterly collection of stories, Elizabeth Jolley has created a splendid array of characters, all of whom fail to achieve the expected. Her stories are sometimes slyly comic, sometimes disturbing – but always they are written with a delicacy and compassion as moving as the characters themselves.

The depth of understanding in her short stories is often disturbing. Sometimes the humour, or the celebration, seems almost a desperate counter to despair and the full burden of that understanding . . .'

Thomas Shapcott, *Westerley*

Elizabeth Jolley's stories are about very simple people, but with deep human sensitivity, and their dreams, though hopeless, put haloes around the contours of everday drabness!

A. R. Chisholm, Melbourne *Age*

The Well

'What have you brought me Hester? What have you brought me from the shop?' 'I've brought Katherine, Father,' Miss Harper said. 'I've brought Katherine, but she's for me.'

Miss Hester Harper, middle aged and eccentric, brings Katherine into her emotionally impoverished life. Together they sew, cook gourmet dishes for two, run the farm, make music and throw dirty dishes down the well.

One night, driving along the deserted track that leads to the farm, they run into a mysterious creature. They heave the body from the roo bar and dump it into the farm's deep well. But the voice of the injured intruder would not be stilled and, most disturbing of all, the closer Katherine is drawn to the edge of the well, the farther away she gets from Hester.

'It is a detective novel without a detective, a thriller without a conclusion . . . a romance and a good read.'

Stephanie Trigg, *Australian Book Review*

'Her fiction shines and shines, like a good deed in a naughty world.'

Angela Carter, *The New York Times Book Review*

Miss Peabody's Inheritance

A middle-aged spinster bound by the demands of her bedridden mother and the routine of her dull office job, Dorothy Peabody has few pleasures in life.

Then she writes a fan letter to an Australian novelist, Diana Hopewell, who to Miss Peabody's delight replies not only with intimate details of her life, but with excerpts from her novel-in-progress. As the correspondence develops, Miss Peabody's total absorption in the fictional adventures of the gently bawdy headmistress, Arabella Thorne, her friends Edgely and Snowdon, and the shy schoolgirl, Gwenda, has startling effects . . .

In this original and very funny novel, Elizabeth Jolley interweaves her two stories so skilfully that the reader, like Miss Peabody, is no longer sure where the boundary between reality and fantasy lies.

'If the hallmark of her writing used to be pathos, it is now irony, even fantasy, so beautifully controlled that the reader is ricocheted between the pitiable, the hilarious and profound in a quite dizzying way'

Washington Post

'Inventively elaborate in its structure and wisely subtle in its tone.'

Options

BOOKS BY JESSICA ANDERSON IN PENGUIN

Tirra Lirra by the River

A beautifully written novel of a woman's seventy-year search to find a place where she truly belongs.

For Nora Porteous, life is a series of escapes. To escape her tightly knit small-town family, she marries, only to find herself confined again, this time in a stifling Sydney suburb with a selfish, sanctimonious husband. With a courage born of desperation and sustained by a spirited sense of humour, Nora travels to London, and it is there that she becomes the woman she wants to be. Or does she?

Winner of the Miles Franklin Award.

Stories from the Warm Zone and Sydney Stories

Jessica Anderson's evocative stories recreate, through the eyes of a child, the atmosphere of Australia between the wars. A stammer becomes a blessing in disguise; the prospect of a middle name converts a reluctant child to baptism. These autobiographical stories of a Brisbane childhood glow with the warmth of memory.

The formless sprawl of Sydney in the 1980s is a very different world. Here the lives of other characters are changed by the uncertainties of divorce, chance meetings and the disintegration and generation of relationships.

Winner of the *Age* Book of the Year Award.

PENGUIN – THE BEST AUSTRALIAN READING

BOOKS BY THEA ASTLEY IN PENGUIN

An Item From the Late News

Wafer, who saw his father blown apart by a bomb in the second world war, and who grew up under the shadow of the nuclear bomb, seeks to spend his middle years in a place of solitude where he can prepare for the inevitable . . .

Allbut, scarcely a dot on the map in the vast Queensland outback, seems to be the perfect place.

But Wafer's peace-loving ways are not understood by the clean and decent locals and when it comes, the final blast is not the one he expected.

It's Raining in Mango

Sometimes history repeats itself.

One family traced from 1860s to the 1980s: from Cornelius to Connie to Reever, who was last seen heading north.

Cornelius Laffey, an Irish born journalist, wrests his family from the easy living of nineteenth-century Sydney and takes them to Cooktown in northern Queensland where thousands of diggers are searching for gold in the mud. The family confront the horror of Aboriginal dispossesion – Cornelius is sacked for reporting the slaughter. His daughter, Nadine, joins the singing whore on the barge and goes upstream, only to be washed out to sea.

The cycles of generations turn, one over the other. Only some things change. That world and this world both have their Catholic priests, their bigots, their radicals. Full of powerful and independent characters, this is an unforgettable tale of the other side of Australia's heritage.

PENGUIN – THE BEST AUSTRALIAN READING

Inner Cities edited by Drusilla Modjeska

How do we imagine our lives and our cities? How do we remember them? Our inner cities. Places shaping people. People shaping places.

A schoolgirl catches the 389 and watches the old women on the bus. Young mothers in the 1950s and 1960s live in the spaces between politics and children. The lives of others are framed by suburban nature strips and inner city footpaths, or the corner house, the corner shop, the kitchen of an Italian restaurant. There are dreams inspired by ships on the harbour or a glimpse of country life. And there are the cultural distances travelled between St Albans and Melbourne University, Redfern and Coraki, Newtown and Greece.

In these essays, stories and poems Australian women write about the places they have lived, the cities they have come to. Their sense of place and space. Geographies real and imagined.

Moments of Desire
edited by Susan Hawthorne and Jenny Pausacker

This feminist anthology ranges widely across women's writing on sex. In fiction, poetry, or experimental forms, the writers unveil a world that few have dared to publicly explore.

The editors have chosen pieces that portray women's sexual experiences as children, adolescents and adults, and the sexual feelings of older women. Some take a humorous approach, others confront the erotic head on.

Sexual alternatives are canvassed; writers explore celibacy, lesbianism, heterosexuality and bisexuality but consistently return to the simple wonders of sensual awareness.

The Glass Whittler Stephanie Johnson

A young woman changes cities, but no one in the new city needs a glass whittler; Robyn, a single mother, buys a house on the proceeds of an unusual business; Nola is fat – one night, reminded of the joys of chocolate by the television she decides to go out – but Nola is locked inside her flat and cannot get out; a retired schoolmistress who has had a stroke is cared for by an alcoholic tramp who has made himself at home in her flat.

Twelve stories by a remarkable young writer. Stephanie Johnson writes about craving for love and companionship, for security and approval of others. The people in these stories seem to find unusual ways of coping with the absurdities and constraints of modern life. But perhaps their solutions are not so strange.

Broken Words Helen Hodgman

Moss wants to go shopping.
Elvis wants an aquarium.
Harold wants to start his own religion.
Princess Anne might want to be left out of it.
Angst wants to know where his next meal is coming from.
Walter and Daphne want Rupert to wake up.
Manny, Maureen and Sue want to open a garage.
Beulah wants the Southern Belle.
Bustler wants to take the baby to Berlin.
Hitler and the Bogeyman want only to be loved.
Le Professeur de Judo wants love to leave him alone.
Renate wants to know what love's got to do with it.
Hazel wants life to have a plot.
But you don't always get what you want . . .

PENGUIN – THE BEST AUSTRALIAN READING

The Hanged Man in the Garden Marion Halligan

The Hanged Man represents a turn around of perception that often occurs when an individual confronts pain. A baby dies, a husband is unfaithful, a woman spends a week in a cupboard, people strive to come to terms with grief and loss – variously they choose humour, despair, irony and hope. It is the unexpectedness of this illogical reversal, that makes the experience precious. And, how ever hard life may be, the sensuous beauty of its surfaces is a source of pleasure.

One of Australia's foremost short story writers, Marion Halligan explores, through the interweaving lives of a group of individuals, the complexities of pain.

West Block Sara Dowse

Canberra's attendant lords look like settling down after a crisis that has rocked Australia. In West Block, the flawed human world behind the headlines, George Harland consummates his career as a public servant; Henry Beeker prepares to fight for a policy; Catherine Duffy confronts the consequences of Australia's Vietnam policy; Jonathan Roe stumbles on happiness; and Cassie Armstrong's ironic intelligence leads her to despair.

But the whispers of a different past move through the rumbling hulk of a building which embodies the history of a capital city and has a future as uncertain as the nation it symbolizes.

Don't Take Your Love to Town Ruby Langford

Ruby Langford is a remarkable woman whose sense of humour has endured through all the hardships she has experienced. Her autobiography is a book which cannot fail to move you.

'I felt like I was living tribal, but with no tribe around me, no close-knit family. The food gathering, the laws and songs were broken up, and my generation at this time wandered around as if we were tribal but in fact living worse than the poorest of poor whites, and in the case of women, living hard because it seemed like the men loved you for a while and then more kids came along and the men drank and gambled and disappeared. One day they'd had enough and they just didn't come back . . .my women friends all have similar stories.'

Born at Box Ridge Mission, Coraki, in the 30s, Ruby Langford's story is one of courage in the face of poverty and tragedy. She writes about the changing ways of life in Aboriginal communities – rural and urban; the distintegration of traditional lifestyles and the sustaining energy that has come from the renewal of Aboriginal culture in recent years.

Canberra Tales

Stories by Margaret Barbalet, Sara Dowse, Suzanne Edgar, Marian Eldridge, Marion Halligan, Dorothy Horsfield, Dorothy Johnston

These stories by seven writers capture the contradictions of life in the nation's capital. They penetrate the glittering surface of a city that is much more than a stamping ground for bureaucrats, diplomats and fat cats. Beneath the sparkle are the shadows of dislocated, sometimes broken lives.

A man enters a strange pact as his daughter lies dying; a young boy makes a ritual of eating around; sadism erupts out of the commonplaces of a broken marriage; revealing stories about the city at the centre of our country's political life and the people whose home it is.

PENGUIN - THE BEST AUSTRALIAN READING

THE PENGUIN AUSTRALIAN WOMEN'S LIBRARY

Series Editor: Dale Spender

The Penguin Australian Women's Library makes available to readers a wealth of information through the work of women writers of our past. It includes the classic to the freshly re-discovered, individual reprints to new anthologies, as well as up-to-date critical re-appraisals of their work and lives as writers.

The Penguin Anthology of Australian Women's Writing edited by Dale Spender

'Only when all the women writers of Australia are brought together is it possible to identify . . . a distinctive female literary tradition.'

Australia has a rich tradition of women writers. In 1790 Elizabeth Macarthur wrote letters home while she travelled to Australia; in 1970 Germaine Greer published *The Female Eunuch*. Thirty-seven writers – working in every genre – are included in this landmark anthology.

Margaret Catchpole, Mary Grant Bruce, Elizabeth Macarthur, Miles Franklin, Georgiana McCrae, Dymphna Cusack, Louisa Ann Meredith, Katharine Susannah Prichard, Catherine Helen Spence, Nettie Palmer, Ellen Clacy, Marjorie Barnard, Mary Fortune (Waif Wander), Eleanor Dark, Ada Cambridge, Dorothy Cottrell, Louisa Lawson, Christina Stead, Jessie Couvreur (Tasma), Sarah Campion, Rosa Praed, Kylie Tennant, Catherine Langloh Parker, Nancy Cato, Barbara Baynton, Faith Bandler, Mary Gaunt, Nene Gare, Mary Gilmour, Olga Masters, Henry Handel Richardson, Oriel Gray, Ethel Turner, Antigone Kefala, G.B. Lancaster, Germaine Greer, Mollie Skinner.

Jungfrau Dymphna Cusack

The options for women in 1936 are limited, but Eve, Marc and Thea are determined – in their very different ways – to cut a place for themselves in the world. Eve is an obstetrician; Thea, contemplating an MA, has an affair with Professor Glover; Marc, thoroughly modern, is a social worker with a special interest in delinquent children. As Eve and Marc watch the progress of Thea's affair the differences between them emerge.

Dymphna Cusack's novel is the first psychological exploration of women's sexuality and aspirations in Australia. Published in 1936 it broke new ground in dealing with issues that had previously been taboo in women's writing. And, it evokes the charm and innocence of Sydney in the years proceeding World War II.

The Fortunes of Mary Fortune edited by Lucy Sussex

Little is known of Mary Fortune. She kept her identity secret by writing under the names of Waif Wander or W.W. Arriving in Australia with her young son she supported herself by writing about life on the goldfields and in the cities. She became Australia's first female writer of crime fiction.

Lucy Sussex's detective work has revealed something of the life of this remarkable woman but her writing is her best testimony. Its verve and quality recreate for the modern reader the harshness of life then, while reflecting many issues still relevant in contemporary society.